Mark moved closer, pressing her into a corner. This wasn't exactly going according to plan. He'd come round to talk to Kate, not to make things ten times worse. But somehow, his hands were slipping round her waist, holding her close. And her hair smelt so wonderful, like oranges and warm sunshine.

'We can't do this,' Kate whispered. 'What about Sarah?' He didn't answer. Instead he kissed her gently. But it was more than just a snog. It made her whole body tingle.

'I wanted to kiss you in the garden,' he said softly, stroking her hair.

Kate nodded. 'Me too.'

She put her hands inside his warm leather jacket, tight around his waist, and kissed him right back.

J-17

Triple Trouble

Just Seventeen

Triple Trouble

The Red-Hot Love Hunt

Too Hot To Handle

Double-Cross Dilemma

Love Games

Girls On Tour

J-17

Triple Trouble

by Anne Harris

RED FOX

A Red Fox Book

Published by Random House Children's Books
20 Vauxhall Bridge Road, London SW1V 2SA

A division of Random House UK Ltd
London Melbourne Sydney Auckland
Johannesburg and agencies throughout the world

1 3 5 7 9 10 8 6 4 2

First published in Great Britain by Red Fox 1997

Typeset in Sabon by
Palimpsest Book Production Limited,
Polmont, Stirlingshire
Printed and bound in Great Britain by
Cox & Wyman Ltd, Reading, Berkshire

Papers used by Random house UK Limited are natural,
recyclable products made from wood grown in sustainable
forests. The manufacturing processes conform to the
environmental regulations of the country of origin.

RANDOM HOUSE UK Limited Reg. No. 954009

ISBN 0 09 925102 7

♥

The Big Snog

Kate followed Joe into the coffee bar, admiring the way his jeans clung to that tight little butt like a jelly mould – mmmmm!

Racing past him, she grabbed a chair and deliberately stretched her long, slim legs onto the nearest coffee table, blocking his path.

'Fancy sharing a slice of pecan pie?' she said, grinning like a maniac. 'You know what they say. Two forks, twice the fun.'

Joe mumbled something under his breath, stepped casually over her legs, and headed for the snack bar.

Unbelievable! Kate chucked her bag at the chair opposite, severely miffed.

It wasn't the first time he'd acted all aloof and blanked her. If she caught his eye in the college refectory, he ducked behind his floppy black hair. Her special lip gloss barely got a smile out of him. She was lucky if he remembered her name. He'd called her Cody twice this week.

Every other lad in the entire sixth form college

was easy snogging-fodder. Kate knew exactly how to grab their attention.

But Mr Cool Computer Guy was playing hard to get. The challenge of the century. Indifferent, independent, and seriously cute with it. Kate leant on her elbows with a sigh, watching him order at the counter.

Those dreamy blue eyes, moody eyebrows, and baby soft skin. Oh to be gorgeous Joe's coffee mug. Caressed by those luscious lips.

The only place she could grab his total attention was on the Internet. Cyber-flirting. For the last two weeks, she'd been sneaking into the computer room, sending him cheeky anonymous messages. But it just wasn't enough.

Kate wanted some real love action. A snog on the information-super-highway was kind of difficult. But tonight, Shelley was having a birthday party. It was going to be huge. And she lived in a big old house, full of cosy snogging corners.

She'd catch Joe in a smoochy mood and . . .

'You owe me a coffee.' Sarah collapsed in a chair beside Kate, blocking her view with a grin. 'Black, no sugar. And no floaty bits on the top.'

Kate leapt up and threw her magazine at Sarah. 'Here, have a go at the Compatibility Quiz. I may be gone some time.'

Kate was never this keen to get coffee. Sarah swivelled round in her chair and saw Joe standing at the counter. Mystery solved. Kate was moving in on him for yet another flirt.

It was embarrassing. Kate flicked her strawberry blonde locks, and twisted his jumper round her fingers, yanking him closer.

If the college ever ran a course in attention seeking, Kate would get a distinction. With honours. And a medal.

And why did she suddenly fancy Joe? Sarah had to admit he was pretty cute, but what about his personality? She wasn't even sure he had one. Without a personality he was just a pair of lips. Kate might as well snog a camel.

Joe walked away from the counter, closely followed by Kate. Sarah grabbed the magazine and pretended to read it.

'So?' Kate shuffled up next to her, coffeeless. 'What do you think of him?'

'He's into computers, right?' Sarah studied his rear view carefully as he walked back to his table. 'Not exactly deep and meaningful. What does he talk about?'

Kate frowned. 'Who cares about conversation? Do you think he's up for a snog?'

'Is that all you want him for? Lip suction?'

'Sarah,' Kate giggled, grabbing the magazine out of her hands. 'It's just a bit of harmless fun.'

Fun. Kate's favourite word. The only thing she took seriously was having a good time.

Sarah peeled off her leather jacket and threw it at her friend. 'Any chance of that coffee? Like sometime today?'

'Only if you're paying.' Kate held out her hand for some money, promising, 'I'll buy next time.'

'Yeah, right. And pigs might fly.' Kate owed her ten coffees and two muffins, at the last count. But even best mates weren't perfect.

Kate came back from the coffee bar with two big mugs and a couple of cookies.

'I've just heard something really interesting,' she said, with a mysterious smile. 'Guess who's going to Shelley's party?'

'Shelley's party, Shelley's party,' Sarah mocked. She was sick of hearing about it. What was so special about a dumb party anyway?

Kate ignored her little outburst. 'I'll give you a clue.' She dunked her cookie in her mug. 'He's tall and scruffy. Never been seen without a guitar . . .'

Sarah squeezed Kate's fingers so tightly that they turned white. 'Mark?' she gasped, quickly checking he wasn't about. 'I thought he was playing a gig tonight at North Street, with the Judas Trees.'

'It's been cancelled.'

'Why?'

'How should I know?' Kate shrugged, rescuing a lump of soggy cookie from the table. 'The manager probably heard them rehearsing.'

Sarah flopped back in her chair. She'd almost decided to skip Shelley's party for a thrilling night in, with a tub of ice-cream and a video. Anything was better than watching Kate drool over Joe.

And PJ, her other best friend, had been acting really weird for weeks. Sarah had no idea why. PJ never shared juicy personal stuff about lads.

But now that Mark was going to the party, she might as well tag along.

She shot up in a sudden panic. 'What am I going to wear?' The Judes wore cool indie clothes. Just the kind of image she was working on for herself – with a touch more colour and style.

'I've gotta go.' She grabbed her art folder. 'Boots shuts in fifteen minutes.'

'What about PJ?' Kate yelled after her.

'She's meeting us there. Eight thirty. Don't be late.'

PJ checked her lipstick in Shelley's bathroom mirror, and messed up her dark bob. Bouncy dance tunes were drifting up through the floorboards from downstairs.

It was nine thirty. Still no sign of Kate and Sarah. Typical. If she stayed in the bathroom until they turned up, the party would be over. And things were beginning to get interesting. So why miss out?

She dodged several snogging couples on the stairs and pushed her way into the kitchen, where some guys from college were toasting their trainers in the microwave. The smell was disgusting – like sweaty popcorn and drains.

She dived straight out again and onto the patio to find Shelley. Or anyone else with a mental age above three and a half.

She didn't see Conrad until he brushed past her, letting his hand linger gently round her waist.

'Hey PJ.' His wide, sexy smile gave her instant goose-bumps. 'Catch you later, maybe?'

'Sure, later,' she smiled back.

The six-foot sport-mad spunk looked even more gorgeous on a footy field in a pair of shorts. Unfortunately, she wasn't the only girl to notice. Half the college would kill to give his muscly legs a quick rub down with a sponge.

Conrad knew it too. He loved the attention. PJ wasn't blind. She'd seen him flirting with his girlie fan club on the touch-line at football practice.

She usually fancied much quieter guys. But what was a girl supposed to do? Ignore that body? Totally out of the question. Especially as she had him all to herself every Tuesday and Thursday morning, in Business Studies. They sat so close together that she could smell his toothpaste.

It would have been easy to scribble her phone number on his folder with a cute message. But PJ had a better plan.

She let him gab about football and laughed at

his dismal jokes. She sussed out his timetable and made certain he caught a quick glimpse of her between classes. Close, but just out of reach.

She left him always wanting more. And it worked. When she walked into a room at college, he noticed. She glanced over her shoulder to see if he was noticing her now. And caught Mish's eye instead.

Mish, super-cow of the sixth form. Mega-bitch extraordinaire. How did she get a party invite?

'So little Miss Sporty Pants . . .' Her obnoxious voice made PJ cringe. 'What's with the sudden interest in footie?' Mish gawped over at Conrad. 'Got anything to do with a certain sexy player?'

PJ shrugged. 'Think what you like.'

Conrad was a secret. Not even Kate and Sarah knew. Mish was just guessing. Trying to stir things up. It was like she had radar or something. It gave PJ the creeps. She ducked past Mish back into the house, before Conrad overheard.

Kate and Sarah were in the hall. About time too. PJ tried to warn them, but it was too late. Mish appeared behind her.

'What on earth is she wearing?' Kate whispered. Crusty old jeans and a tiny top, with her belly trapped between the two. Like when you bite into a vanilla slice and the custard squirts out.

'Gross!' Sarah gasped.

Mish tossed her shiny black bob, laughing loudly at Kate's skimpy frock. 'I didn't know this was a fancy-dress party.'

'So why did you come as Dracula?' Kate snapped.

Mish barged past them up the stairs. 'Doesn't she ever take a break from bitching?' Sarah hissed.

'Only when there's a full moon,' PJ giggled. 'And then she turns into a vampire bat.'

'Nothing that a personality transplant wouldn't fix,' Kate chipped in, adjusting her boots. 'Is Joe here yet?'

PJ pointed to the lounge. 'Last seen heading for the snacks.'

'Perfect.' Kate smoothed a long stray hair into place, grinning like a cat about to get the cream. 'I'm going after him. Wish me luck, girls.'

'Luck's got nothing to do with it,' Sarah whispered. PJ had to agree. When Kate fancied a lad, he didn't stand a chance.

Kate peered round the heaving lounge. Joe looked even more luscious than usual in jeans and a plain long-sleeved top. She intended to grab him quickly. Before somebody else did.

She pushed past the footy team and sat next to him on the sofa. It was a tight squeeze. Just the way Kate liked it.

'Great party,' she yelled above the thumping house music. He nodded and turned towards her.

'Not enough food.' Typical lad reaction. Stomach first. Snogging later.

He suddenly leant closer, holding his floppy hair out of his gorgeous blue eyes. Maybe he was going to say something cute after all. Like, 'Kate, I need you. I can't fight it any longer. Take me on that lurve train to Snog City Central.' Fat chance.

'I'm going on a food hunt,' he shouted in her ear. 'Want to come, Cody?'

She thumped him hard on the arm. 'It's Kate, Dumbo.'

Ready and willing? Joe wasn't even lukewarm. What did a girl have to do?

PJ left Sarah talking to her arty mates at the top of the stairs. Conrad had promised to catch her later. Well, it was later now, and PJ was ready to be caught.

She wandered onto the balcony at the back of Shelley's bedroom. She could see the whole massive garden below. But no sign of Conrad.

She'd left it too late. He'd already gone home, probably with another girl.

'Looking for someone special?'

'Conrad!' she gasped spinning round. 'Don't ever try that again.'

'Sorry.' He wasn't sorry at all. 'What are you

doing up here all alone? You missed the balloon basketball match.'

'I'm heartbroken,' she smiled, sneaking a quick look at his amazing profile.

He even had a sporty face, as if he'd just stepped out of a high tech trainers ad. Big brown eyes, square jaw, cute nose and snog-friendly lips. Even his cropped brown hair was perfect.

He moved closer for a quick arm fondle. 'Come and watch me play for real sometime. I'll show you my slam dunk.'

'Great.' PJ hated sport. But she could learn to like it. 'I'll leave a space free in my diary,' she laughed, suddenly shivering.

Conrad took off his denim jacket, and put it over her clingy blue dress. 'It looks kind of cute on you.'

It was toasty and warm too. She could even smell his delicious aftershave. Pity he wasn't inside it with her. Still, at least now she could get a better look at those shoulders.

PJ wondered if she should mention that her lips were a tad chilly too, just to see if he offered to resuscitate them. But before she could speak, he slipped his arm smoothly round her shoulders, and suddenly, they were in lip-lock – dry roasted peanut flavour.

Conrad snogged like he played footy, straight in for a clean tackle, no hesitation.

'It's cold out here,' he grinned when they came up for air. 'Let's go in for a dance. And keep each other warm.'

So everyone could see them together? PJ preferred copping off in private. But Conrad was already through the balcony doors, expecting her to follow.

Kate glanced around the room. Conditions were perfect. The lounge was dark, cramped and sweaty. She'd persuaded Joe to dance. His body language was finally sending out imminent snog signals. One last nudge in the right direction and he'd be all hers.

She grabbed his top with both hands and pulled him closer. 'So how much longer do we have to smooch before you kiss me?' She brushed his lips gently.

'Kate . . .' He hesitated, then kissed her back. A full tongue sarnie. It was worth the wait. For a computer guy he was a pretty cool kisser.

'I've got numb lips.' He grinned down at her, floppy hair hiding his eyes. 'But it feels kind of nice.'

At last she had him. Exactly where she wanted him. Wrapped snugly around her little finger.

'Mission accomplished?' PJ suddenly appeared at her shoulder. Holding hands with Conrad! Kate guided Joe backwards to get a closer look at the happy couple, and trod accidentally on Mish.

'Watch it, big bum.'

'A mate of yours?' Joe laughed.

Kate ignored her. She had more important things on her mind. Like PJ's new snogging partner.

She twirled Joe round until she was dancing back to back with her friend.

'When did this little love match kick off?' she hissed.

'I'll tell you later,' PJ teased. 'Where did Sarah get to?'

Kate shrugged. 'I thought she was with you?'

Sarah sat on the edge of the patio. The whole party had been a total disaster. Some moron had flicked greasy mayonnaise in her carefully arranged hair, and all down her expensive new skirt. And Mark hadn't even bothered to show up.

She'd had a feeling about tonight too. A sort of sixth sense that something amazing was going to happen. So much for instincts.

She walked down the garden, heading for the summer-house with its rainbow fairy lights.

But somebody had beaten her to it. A figure darted for cover in the shadows as she opened the door.

'Who's there?' she whispered, getting ready to

run. Suddenly, she knew exactly who was lurking in the darkness. Nobody else smelt like patchouli oil and chewing gum but Mark.

'Sarah?' His voice was unmistakable too. Laid-back and teasing.

'Come in quick, and close the door. I'm hiding.'

'Who from?' Sarah crouched away from the light outside.

'Samantha. My ex.'

She could see him now. Sprawled across a bench with his bass guitar – he never went anywhere without it. He was wearing his usual scruffy jeans and a shirt that was way too small. Perfect bass player clothes. It gave him that super-sexy, just crawled out of bed look.

'I was working on a new song for the Judes.' He grinned, strumming his guitar lazily. 'Great poster you did for our last gig, by the way. The rest of the band loved it. Want to do another one?'

'Sure. If I can squeeze it in.' Squeeze it in. Ha! She'd work on it day and night until it was perfect. 'I should probably come and watch you rehearse again.' She unbuttoned her leather jacket, showing off her new skimpy top. 'To get new poster ideas . . .'

Another two whole hours with the Judes. Heaven in a rehearsal room. Just like last time. Staring at Mark's sexy green eyes and long dark lashes.

'Any requests?' he patted his bass, giving her a

♥ 13 ♥

cheeky, flirty grin that made her stomach flip over backwards.

She could think of several requests. And they weren't all songs.

'Make something up. A love song.'

Mark looked uneasy. 'You mean like a ballad?' He started picking out random notes and playing around with clumsy words.

Sarah listened in a dream. She'd been doing her homework on Mark. His birthday was on February 10th. Which made him an individual, creative Aquarius. Bubbly, with a gentle, sensitive hidden side. Full of deep feelings and searching questions. And everyone knew bass players wrote the best songs, right?

What Mark needed was a cool Taurus rock-chick to help him cope with the stresses of stardom. He could drive her to gigs in his car. Write her songs. And everyone would know she was part of the Judas Tree crowd. Mark's girlfriend.

He stopped playing suddenly, stroking his stubbly chin. 'Composing's kind of tricky if you're not in the right mood. Fancy a walk instead?'

There was a path behind the summer-house, running along the dark bushes at the bottom of the garden.

'This is so spooky,' Sarah whispered. 'Like everything's alive.'

The moonlight made strange shapes and giant shadows. She edged closer to Mark for safety. Only suddenly Mark wasn't there. Sarah stopped and listened.

'Mark?' she called, self-consciously. 'This isn't funny. Where are you?'

Total scary silence. She jumped as the bush beside her started rustling and making ghostly sounds. A hand reached out and dragged her through the matted twigs and leaves.

'Gotcha!' laughed Mark, pinning her gently against a tree and kissing her. Twice. Long and lingering. Exactly the way she'd imagined. Total snog heaven. Olympic standard.

He stopped abruptly, checking his watch.

'Uh-oh! Band meeting. I forgot. I should have been there twenty minutes ago.' He kissed her quickly and tumbled out of the bushes.

'Wait!' Sarah yelled. He didn't even have her phone number.

She scrambled back into the garden, trying not to snag her clothes. But he'd already disappeared into the house. Great.

What happened now? Did they ignore each other at college on Monday? Act like strangers? Pretend it never happened? Or start dating?

Sarah sighed, completely confused. Monday morning was going to take a century to arrive.

♥

Dating Games

'Guess what I've got in my pocket?' Sarah skipped over Kate's legs and sat on the coffee table, grinning from ear to ear.

'The money you owe me from the other night?' said PJ, hopefully.

Sarah ignored her. 'I'll give you a clue.' She pulled a tiny scrap of paper out of her jacket.

'It's a shopping list,' yawned Kate. 'So what?'

Sarah thumped her on the leg.

'Ow! What was that for?'

'It's not a shopping list, stupid, it's a love letter.'

'Oh my God!' Kate shrieked, squashing up on the table beside her. 'From Mark?'

'Who else?' Sarah waved it teasingly in front of her face. 'But you probably don't want to hear what it says.'

'Just try me.' Kate snatched it out of her hands. 'Where's the rest of it? You said it was a letter, this is barely a note.'

Sarah always exaggerated. She couldn't just have

a headache, it had to be a brain tumour. Kate cleared her throat and read the note out loud.

'Friday night in the bushes was amazing. Meet me outside college today, four o'clock. Mark.' Kate folded it up again, teasing, 'What were you two doing in the bushes? Bird watching?'

'Just talking.' Sarah picked at Kate's toasted peanut butter bagel with a secretive smile. 'Maybe I should go home now? I've got to find something to wear for tonight.'

'You've only just had breakfast,' Kate frowned, moving her plate before Sarah scoffed the lot.

'So? Is there a law against looking stunning on a first date?'

Sarah leant back against the wall. She pressed Mark's note to her nostrils. It smelt of patchouli oil. If she closed her eyes she could feel him kissing her all over again.

PJ rolled her eyes at Kate. It was useless trying to talk to Sarah when she had that dreamy look. You could get more sense out of a Blue Peter pet.

'What's happening with Joe?' she asked Kate instead. 'Are you two officially an item now?'

'I'm meeting him tonight for a pizza.'

'In a restaurant?' Sarah sat up, suddenly back in the real world. 'That means he'll actually have to talk to you. Like in sentences.'

'Joe and I have a deep and spiritual connection,' Kate joked. 'We don't need words.'

'Just breath mints and saliva.' PJ chucked her a stick of chewing gum.

'Do you think pizza's kind of dull for a first date?' Kate sighed.

'Pizza's perfect, you have to go,' said Sarah, producing a magazine from her bag. 'Just listen to your horoscope. "Scorpio," she read. "Today Venus, the planet of love, is partying hard in your sign. Sparks fly at a lunch or dinner date, leaving you in no doubt about your true feelings." See,' she shoved the page under Kate's nose, 'pizza is your destiny.'

'So what does mine say?' PJ asked eagerly, pointing to the Libra Lovescope.

'You love to share your thoughts and emotions.' Sarah paused. A clam was more willing to share its feeling than PJ. 'But a special Sagittarian lad wants to get to know you too well. Take care! This boy's trouble. Confide in your friends instead – it's much safer.'

'Confide in your friends,' Kate repeated, tugging at PJ's sleeve. 'You have to tell us about Conrad now. It's in the stars.'

'And I did let you read my love letter.' Sarah grabbed PJ's bag, holding it hostage. 'You're not getting this back until you give us details.'

'Actually,' sighed PJ, pinching the rest of Kate's bagel, 'there is something important you should all know.' She put her arms around both of them and whispered, 'Conrad isn't a Sagittarian.'

She escaped over the back of the chairs, grabbing her bag, and dived out of the coffee bar,
giggling.

Conrad would be waiting for her in Business
Studies. She'd met him once that morning already,
at eight o'clock, in a greasy spoon café for
breakfast.

She'd walked in and caught him admiring his
own reflection in the cutlery.

'Have you ever noticed how big your nose looks
in the back of a spoon?' he'd said, checking it from
different angles.

'You know what they say,' she'd said. 'Fat head,
big nose.'

God, he was so vain! She couldn't resist a quick
tease. He didn't know how to handle it. Conrad
might be good at sports, but she was an expert in
other kinds of games.

He'd ordered Danish pastries and coffee, and
found them a private little table at the back of the
café. He could be quite sweet – when he tried. He'd
even brought her a present. A tiny plastic elephant
on a shoe lace.

'It cost me a fortune,' he'd grinned, tying it
round her wrist like a charm bracelet.

'You mean it fell out of a cereal packet.'

'OK,' he'd laughed. 'But it took me hours to
choose a matching shoe lace.'

She checked it was still round her wrist. He'd

made her promise to wear it twenty-four hours a day. Maybe he gave them to all his girlfriends, like a sort of identity bracelet?

The Business Studies room was in chaos as usual. Conrad was already there, looking totally delicious in a warm, huggable jumper, still rubbing sleep out of his eyes.

He brushed her arm with his fingers as she sat down, making her skin tingle.

'Have you missed me?' he yawned, sleepily.

'Since breakfast?' PJ pinched his leg. 'I think I could have survived until lunch-time.'

He grinned, stretching his arm around the back of her chair. 'I've got a footie match tomorrow night. Come and watch me play?' He didn't have time for a real date. And PJ would look cute on the touchline.

'I might,' PJ shrugged. 'If you're lucky.'

A whole ninety minutes of Conrad's legs. She'd be there early, with plasters and massage oil. What else were girlfriends for, right?

Sarah stood outside college at the end of afternoon lessons, giving her lashes a quick touch of mascara. She read her horoscope again.

'Taurians,' it said. 'Be prepared for the night of your life! This guy is crazy about you and he's not afraid to show it.'

He might be crazy about her, but he was also nineteen minutes late. She seemed to spend her entire life just waiting for Mark to show up.

At least he wasn't avoiding her. She felt for the patchouli scented note in her pocket. He'd slipped it into her locker before lessons. Typical male Aquarian behaviour – deeply romantic, once he'd found the right girl.

'Hey, Sarah.' He was here at last. Driving up in an old blue convertible with the hood down. It was definitely the kind of car you got noticed in.

'Am I late?'

Late, but incredibly cute. She'd forgiven him already.

'I've only just got here too,' Sarah shrugged. 'I thought you might have gone without me.'

OK, so it was a lie. But rock-chicks were always late. And she had her image to consider.

'Jump in.' He patted the maroon leather seat with a mischievous grin. 'The door doesn't open so you'll have to climb over.'

That wasn't easy in a long dress, not without half the world catching a glimpse of her knickers.

'Sorry about the party. I shouldn't have abandoned you in the bushes.'

'Don't worry.' She bumped onto the seat beside him. 'You can make it up to me now.'

'Sure.' He stared at her over his shades with a dangerous smile. 'I'll take you somewhere really special.'

A moonlit walk along the beach? Or a wild night out with the Judes maybe? Mark was the baby of the band. The rest of the guys had already left college. They probably knew loads of cool clubs and places just to hang out and be seen.

They cruised out of the gates past a couple of her mates from Art class. Perfect timing. By tomorrow morning, it would be all over the college. Sarah and Mark – a match made in heaven. Item of the year.

She sighed happily and shuffled up closer to Mark and his exclusive Judas Tree T-shirt, just as he pulled into the city ice-rink car park.

'This is it,' he beamed at her.

It had to be a joke. Lads in bands gatecrashed parties, they acted cool at clubs, gigs and rehearsals. But ice-skating?

'We're meeting the Judes inside?' she asked hopefully.

'No.' He gave her hand a quick squeeze. 'Tonight it's just you and me.'

And two hundred other skaters. Very intimate. She had hoped he'd take her somewhere a little more mature, so that they could talk.

She fastened her boots as slowly as she could,

watching Mark showing off on his skates. He was good at it. Confident, unafraid. He stopped beside her, breathless, taking both her cold hands in his, with a teasing smile.

'Now it's your turn. Don't worry,' he promised. 'I won't let you fall.'

He always brought first dates to the rink. It was a great way of getting physical without getting slapped in the face. And he'd like to get to know Sarah a lot better. She was a great looking girl. Beautiful almond shaped eyes, long, straight, shiny hair . . .

'You're a natural,' he smiled, gripping her elbows as she skidded dangerously.

'Liar,' she giggled.

Her feet were out of control, supermarket trolley style. If Mark let go of her now, she'd be on her butt, in a puddle, totally humiliated. But she was suddenly so close to him that she didn't really care.

He drove her home right through the centre of town with the hood down, singing along to a tape of the Judes last gig. He had a seriously sexy voice. It sent little shivers all down her body.

'Why don't you sing on stage?' she yelled above the noise of the car.

'The other guys won't let me. Too afraid of the competition,' he beamed.

'So start your own band?'

'Nah,' shrugged Mark. 'I like being in the Judes. We're rehearsing some of my new songs tomorrow night. Come and listen.'

'I'll bring my camera,' she nodded. 'Get some shots for the new gig poster.' And a few private snaps for her own collection.

'How are your ankles?' he shouted.

Puffing up like two inflatable life-rafts. But it was worth the pain. They hadn't done much talking, but kissing on ice – wow! Every girl should try it! It was unbelievably exciting.

She couldn't wait to give Kate and PJ the juicy details.

Joe was waiting outside Pizza Palace, with a big smile. He should smile more often, Kate thought. He looked kind of sweet with dimples.

She crossed the road slowly, letting him get a good long look at her clingy new shirt.

'I hope those lips are ready for another snogging session.' She stopped before him, touching his face gently.

'I can't make any promises, Kate.' He'd remembered her name. Amazing. 'Shall we go in?'

'What's the big rush?' She grabbed him round the waist and pulled him into a shadowy shop doorway. 'You should never eat pizza with cold lips. It gives you indigestion. Didn't they teach you that in biology?'

Joe shook his head. 'I would have remembered.' He kissed her softly.

'Urgh! Joe!' she gasped, pushing him away. 'What have you been eating?'

'I had some garlic bread for lunch . . .'

'Well, kissing is definitely off the menu,' she sighed, reapplying her lipstick. She hated garlic.

Sarah was right. They'd have to talk to each other instead. Still, maybe there was more to Joe than floppy hair and warm lips. He could turn out to be her perfect man. And it was a good opportunity to ask some personal questions. Starting with details about his ex-girlfriends.

'So are the rumours true?' she said, as the waiter showed them to a table in the corner of Pizza Palace. 'About you, Janey and the last bus home from town?'

'Who told you that?' Joe looked embarrassed. 'Don't believe everything you hear.'

Typical. Lads could gabble on for hours about football and cars, but when it came to previous snogging partners, they were useless.

'Well, we have to talk about something.' She squeezed onto the seat beside him, playing with his shiny hair. 'Tell me what you know about Conrad and Mark.'

'Nothing,' Joe shrugged, picking up a menu.

OK, so he didn't want to talk. Non-verbal communication could be just as much fun. More, if she did it right.

She slipped off her sandal, and tickled his bony ankle with her bare toes.

Joe blushed and looked round in a panic. 'Kate, what are you doing?'

'Checking for a pulse,' she teased, trying out his other ankle.

He squirmed out of reach. Kate was drop dead gorgeous, but sometimes she went way over the top.

'I don't believe it,' Kate hissed, suddenly ducking behind a menu.

Mish, the bitch from hell, was heading straight for their table. Black hair flying like a witch on broomstick. Why couldn't she go and ruin somebody else's date?

'So . . .' Mish pulled up a chair and sat down, helping herself to a bread stick. 'You two are an item now?'

'Yeah, and three's a crowd,' Kate snapped. 'So if you've finished being nosey . . .'

She gave them a sickly smile. 'Sorry, didn't know I was interrupting.'

'Sure you did,' Kate sighed. Mish was one long interruption in her life. 'Who are you here with anyway?' she asked. 'An imaginary friend?'

'One of your ex-boyfriends, actually. But then

♥ 26 ♥

you've had so many, you probably don't recognise faces.'

Kate gave her a sarcastic smile. 'You're just jealous because I can get a date without using a blindfold.'

'Yeah, right.' Mish stood up, blowing out the candle on their table. 'Save it for someone who thinks you're funny.'

What was it Kate's horoscope had said? 'Sparks fly at a dinner date?' She'd been saving her sparks for Joe. But with sour face Mish hanging around, romance was impossible.

Maybe Joe would loosen up on a group date? Kate had the perfect place in mind.

'You realise we could get arrested for doing this,' Sarah grinned, wriggling into a comfy position on her beach towel. 'Your two minutes are up.' She grabbed the toy binoculars out of Kate's hands. 'It's my turn.'

Kate had bought the binoculars in town. 'To study wildlife at the beach.' Sarah should have guessed she wasn't talking about seagulls and jellyfish. Mark, Joe and Conrad were the only life forms they'd been studying.

'Are the lads still playing volleyball?' Kate lay back in the warm sand, soaking up some sun.

'Joe's serving. Conrad's moving in for a point.

No wait . . .' Sarah giggled, excitedly, 'he's taking his top off.'

'Oh my God!' Kate shrieked crawling onto Sarah's towel. 'Let me see.'

PJ squeezed in between them both. Conrad was always going topless. At footie matches and basketball practice – any excuse to get his pectorals out in public.

'Conrad's so brown,' Kate sighed. Joe was more of a pinky colour. And Mark was so luminous white that he could warn shipping off the rocks at night.

'Has Mark written you a ballad yet?' Kate jabbed Sarah playfully in the arm. 'Or have you been too busy exploring each other's dental work?'

'What do you think?' giggled Sarah.

Mark had played three of his new songs at rehearsals the other day. 'Shock-a-holics', 'Head Shrinker', and 'Aliens Shop at Spaceways.'

Not exactly ballad material. But it was early days yet. And sensitive love songs couldn't be rushed.

'Conrad's won the game,' PJ informed them, munching on an apple. 'Joe's laughing about something. I thought you said he was quiet, Kate?' She sat up suddenly in a panic. 'Quick, they're coming back. What do I do with these?'

Kate grabbed the binoculars and hid them under her beach towel. Just in time.

'Hey, girls!' Mark collapsed in the sand beside them, looking hot and sweaty. 'What's the big joke?'

'You wouldn't believe me if I told you,' said Kate, pushing the binoculars discreetly into the sand with her elbow.

'Anyone fancy walking up the beach for an ice-cream?' Conrad towered above them. 'Joe lost the game so he's paying.'

Sarah grabbed her shades. 'You've twisted my arm.'

Kate watched them wandering along the water's edge. No wonder PJ fancied Conrad. With a body like that, who cared if he had brains? You could spend weeks admiring his leg muscles, before worrying about little things like mental ability.

'You and Joe went to that new club in town last night?' Mark said, interrupting her thoughts. 'What's it like?'

'Wild and crazy,' she joked.

Actually, they'd left well before midnight. Joe hated the music. And his dancing . . . She'd never seen anything like it. Face frowning, buttocks clenched, as if he'd found wet sand in his boxers.

'Has Sarah done your rune stones yet?' Kate yawned, propping herself up on one elbow to face Mark.

'No.' He looked worried. 'Does it hurt?'

'That depends,' chipped in PJ, winking at Kate, 'on the size of the runes.'

Mark nodded, rubbing sand out of his hair. 'And does she always go on about dreams and stuff?'

'Always,' Kate giggled. 'She says dreams can unravel your deepest secrets and desires.'

Mark tried to hide a smile. 'Mine don't need much unravelling.'

Kate could believe it. Mark was easier to read than alphabetti spaghetti. When he looked at Sarah he was either confused or horny.

He lay back in the sand, covering his face with his T-shirt. 'Wake me up when it's time to go.'

As soon as he'd closed his eyes, PJ sprawled out alongside Kate.

'You haven't said much about Joe?' she whispered. 'Is everything OK with you two?'

Kate shrugged. 'I guess so. He's just a bit . . .'

It was difficult to explain. Joe was so good-looking, and a fantastic kisser. It had taken her weeks to grab his attention. But now that she had him, she wasn't really sure she wanted him.

'Kate?' PJ was watching her, concerned. 'What's wrong?'

'Nothing.' She took a bite out of PJ's apple and rolled onto her back. 'Joe's a real cutie.'

But was he cute enough?

♥

The Wrong Guy

'I feel sick,' Kate groaned, clutching her stomach. 'Who's idea was it to stay in and pig-out anyway?'

'Yours,' Sarah chucked a cushion at her head.

'Next time I have a bright idea, shoot me, OK? I never want to see another chocolate brownie again.'

'Popcorn anyone?' PJ wandered into the lounge carrying a large bowl.

Kate moaned loudly and buried her face in the carpet. 'Take it away before I throw up.'

PJ grinned, wedging the bowl between two cushions on the sofa.

'So what did we score in the Friendship Quiz?' asked Sarah.

PJ picked up her magazine. 'We all got over thirty points. Which means . . .,' she flicked over the page, 'we're in group A. A Trusting Triangle.'

Kate rolled onto her stomach. 'Any relation to the Bermuda Triangle?'

'Shut up and listen for once in your life,' PJ nudged Kate with her foot, and carried on reading. 'Your three-way friendship is based on a mutual respect and understanding of each other's feelings . . .'

'. . . and a keen interest in lads,' Sarah interrupted.

'Not according to this,' PJ grinned. 'But it does say we'll be friends for all eternity, and beyond.'

'Scary thought,' Sarah teased, crawling across the floor, collapsing in an empty chair. 'Do you realise, we've been together in the same room for three whole hours, and nobody's mentioned boyfriends yet?'

'Yeah,' grinned PJ. 'Why don't you ask me about Conrad?'

'Is there any point?' asked Sarah. 'Would you actually tell us anything if we did?'

PJ considered it for a second, then grabbed another handful of popcorn, giggling, 'No.'

Kate sat up hugging her knees. 'Can we talk about something else for a change? Anything but chocolate brownies and boyfriends.'

'Quick, call an ambulance,' Sarah laughed, feeling her forehead for signs of fever and delirium. 'You talk about boyfriends like constantly, Kate.'

'Usually somebody else's,' said PJ, chucking popcorn at her. That was one of the reasons why PJ never told Kate anything personal. She had ears like a bat, and a mouth the size of Merseyside.

Kate switched on the TV. 'Well, tonight I don't want to, OK?'

If they talked about boyfriends, she'd have to discuss Joe. She was supposed to be with him now. Playing pool. But she'd faked a headache and escaped to PJ's instead.

She couldn't take any more. Joe might have the best bum in town, but he was so dull. He lived on planet boring. What had happened to the sexy lad she'd snogged at Shelley's party? After their first real date, he'd crawled back into his shell and pulled down the blinds. She'd made a huge mistake. Wasted weeks of valuable snogging time. She should have dumped him ages ago.

But things were not that simple. She'd got a bit carried away, told Sarah and PJ that Joe was the most fantastic guy she'd ever dated. If she dumped him now, Sarah would accuse her of being shallow. PJ probably thought she was anyway.

And she didn't want to hurt Joe. He might win boring boyfriend of the century award, but basically he was a nice guy. Kate sighed. Her life was in a total mess.

'Anyone want to watch the late night horror film?' PJ asked, making herself comfortable on the sofa.

Kate sat next to her. 'I've got a better idea. Let's phone Mish, and tell her that Joe's been in love with her for months.' It was the quickest way of getting rid of any lad.

'We can't,' said PJ. 'There's a full moon tonight. She'll be out sucking blood.'

Sarah frowned. 'How could you even think about doing that to Joe?'

'It was only a joke.' Kate flopped back against the cushions as the phone began to ring.

PJ jumped up and sprinted into the hall to answer it. Conrad usually rang at about this time. When Kate was in a giddy mood, it was safer not to let her anywhere near a phone.

'Hey, PJ. What's going on?' Conrad sounded sleepy. You could tell a lot about a lad by his voice. Sometimes Conrad's voice was so gentle and smooth, as if behind the sporty guy image there was someone totally different – someone special? Then he'd start waffling about footie and ruin the whole effect.

'It sounds like you're having a party,' he yawned.

'It's just Kate and Sarah messing around,' PJ mumbled.

They were peering round the door at her now, giggling like two maniacs. Kate was snogging a cushion, making stupid kissing noises, calling it Conrad. 'Idiots,' she smiled, pushing the door shut with her foot.

'You three having a night in?' Conrad suddenly sounded interested. 'Have you been talking about me?'

'Yeah, but we got bored and moved onto Mark,' PJ teased. 'He's a really interesting guy.'

'Oh yeah?' Conrad was so easy to wind up. 'Well, maybe I should call round and liven things up?'

'Sure. If you don't mind trying out lipsticks and wearing a pink nightie.'

'Pink's not really my colour,' he laughed. 'Listen, I've got a match tomorrow. Come and watch, and we could go for a Chinese afterwards.'

PJ rolled her eyes. Conrad didn't understand her at all. Just because she was quiet and cute, he assumed she was a soft touch. Doormat material.

He never took her on a proper date. Just squeezed her in for breakfast, or a quick take-away between matches. He expected her to play the faithful, loving girlfriend. Smiling sweetly at his mates.

Well, it was getting kind of tedious. She had a life too.

'So how about it?' Conrad yawned. 'The Chinese, tomorrow?'

'OK,' she sighed reluctantly. 'I have to go.' Kate and Sarah had probably emptied her bag by now and found her diary. 'I'll see you tomorrow at the match.'

She put the phone down and wandered back into the lounge. If he'd had bandy legs and a flat bottom, she'd have dumped him weeks ago. But she wasn't finished with that gorgeous body yet.

Sarah had pinched her seat on the sofa. 'Does Conrad phone you every single night?'

'I think it's sweet.' Kate gave PJ a friendly hug. 'Have you set a date for the wedding yet?'

'Very funny.' PJ picked up the popcorn and wafted it under Kate's nose. 'Boyfriends are a banned subject, remember? He was ringing to tell me about tomorrow's football match.'

'Football?' Kate's eyes lit up. 'Can we come and keep you company?'

PJ shrugged. 'Why not?'

'Football's boring,' Sarah yawned.

'Who cares about the game?' Kate tutted. Sometimes Sarah could be so dense. 'I'm interested in the legs.'

'Well, why didn't you say so?' Sarah smiled. Football might not be such a total drag after all. 'So what do I wear to a match?'

'Mascara,' said Kate, stretching out along the floor and grinning.

'Don't you go to watch Mark's band rehearsing on a Wednesday?' PJ asked.

Sarah put her feet up on the arm of the sofa with a long sigh. 'He can manage without me for once.'

The best way to get rid of Joe without actually dumping him, Kate decided, was to keep out of his way. Let things fizzle out naturally. No more dull dates with Mr Pizza.

Phase one, the next morning, was making it past the Computer room without being spotted.

She turned into the main corridor. So far so good. Lessons had already started, the walkway was almost empty. If she could just get to English . . . Joe suddenly appeared out of nowhere, striding towards her.

She had to move fast. She dived quickly into the boys' toilets, with her eyes semi-closed, just in case. And walked straight into a familiar Judas Tree T-shirt.

'Kate?' Mark held her steady, staring in disbelief. 'What are you doing in here?'

There was a wicked gleam in Kate's eyes. She was the kind of girl who'd burst in and embarrass you with a polaroid camera, just for the hell of it.

'You've got to hide me from Joe.' Kate glanced in a panic over her shoulder. 'He's right behind me.'

Mark brushed a hand through his scruffy hair. 'You two had an argument?'

'Not yet.'

Mark grabbed her sleeve and pulled her into a grotty-looking cubicle, locking the door behind them. 'We should be safe in here.'

There was barely room to breathe with the two

of them squashed in together like sardines. 'Mark,' Kate whispered. '*You* don't need to hide. I'm the one who's escaping from Joe, remember?'

'Yeah, but this way it's more exciting.' He jiggled his eyebrows wickedly.

'What if we get caught?' Swapping air space with her best mate's boyfriend in the lads' inner sanctum. Gossip like that spread round college like wildfire.

'Getting caught's half the fun,' grinned Mark.

She couldn't help smiling back. Mark was a laugh. He wrote his own rules. Why couldn't Joe be like that?

'Are you OK?' he hissed, shuffling to one side. Kate's elbows were digging into his ribs.

Kate nodded. 'How's the band?'

'Great, we've got a big gig coming up soon. Sarah's doing the posters. You and Joe should come and hear us play.'

Kate cringed. She wouldn't be taking Joe. Not if she wanted to have some fun anyway.

'The guys might even let me sing a couple of songs this time,' he grinned excitedly.

'Thanks for the warning,' she whispered. 'Remind me to take my earplugs, just in case.'

The outside door banged shut, making them both jump. Kate froze. What if it was Joe?

'Stay still,' Mark hissed, standing on the toilet seat, and slowly peering over the top of the cubicle.

'It must have been the college ghost,' he grinned down at her. 'The coast's clear.'

Kate let out a sigh of relief and unlocked the door. Now she was here, she might as well take a look around. She'd always wondered what it was like.

It was much bigger than the girls' toilets, with plenty of mirror space too.

She'd expected a swamp. Flooded floors, toilet paper hanging from the water pipes, like jungle creepers in a Tarzan movie. Mysterious, toxic smells radiating round the room. But it wasn't that bad. Quite clean in fact. Considering.

'I was on my way to the coffee bar.' Mark leant on a wash basin as she checked her lipstick in the mirrors. 'Do you fancy sharing a doughnut?'

'Sure. Let's go.'

The quicker the better. The boys' toilets wasn't exactly the social spot of the month.

Kate followed him back into the corridor, hiding behind his leather jacket until she was certain that Joe had disappeared.

'So when do I get to see round the girls' toilets?' Mark joked.

Kate shrugged, flicking a speck of dandruff off his shoulder with a flirty smile. 'Whenever Sarah can take you, I guess.'

*

'How much longer are they going to play?' Sarah sighed, folding her arms in a huff. 'Haven't they had enough yet?'

'See that tall guy over there in the track suit?' Kate pointed to the referee. 'Go complain to him and give my ears a rest.'

Sarah had been a total pain since the footie match had started. Moaning about the wet grass, asking dumb questions.

So it wasn't exactly an exciting game. One feeble goal and a pitch invasion by a stray dog were the only highlights so far. But was that her fault?

'I could have been out shopping for a new eyeliner, instead of watching this stupid game,' said Sarah, sulkily, getting her walkman out of her bag.

Kate nudged her playfully. 'Don't let me stop you. The shops are still open.'

'What and leave you here alone?' Sarah almost smiled. 'It's too risky. If Conrad takes his shirt off, you'll probably pass out.'

Besides, being with Kate stopped her brooding over Mark. It wasn't as if they'd split up or anything. She still liked being with him. After all, he was part of the coolest band in town.

But she'd given up searching for his sensitive, creative side. Mark didn't have one. He was about as deep as a bird bath. He never even came near the Art room to look at her work. It was as if he was afraid of catching something.

And they'd had their first argument the other night. About band rehearsals.

It was so boring. She just stared out of the window like a zombie, while the Judes played 'Aliens Shop at Spaceways,' a million times, over and over. It was driving her crazy.

Where was all the glamour and excitement? What about the wild parties and the paparazzi? How could she show off her new rock-chick trousers if they were cooped up in a dusty, stinky attic overlooking the college dustbins?

'So don't come if you're bored,' Mark had said, when she'd complained about the lack of action.

'Are you saying you don't want me here?'

'If you can't stand the heat,' he'd shrugged, 'stay out of the rehearsal room.'

'Fine, if that's the way you want it.' She'd grabbed her bag and stormed out in a temper.

He'd phoned her later to apologise, of course. But from now on, she'd decided to give Wednesday night rehearsals a miss – that was why she was here, watching football.

Life would get more exciting when the Judes came out of hibernation and actually played a gig. But it had better be soon.

'I guess PJ's not going to turn up now,' Kate checked her watch. 'This isn't like her at all. She asked us to come and keep her company.'

'You invited yourself,' Sarah reminded her.

Kate nodded. 'Same thing.'

Something wasn't right. PJ was the reliable one. She was never late for anything. What was she up to, Kate wondered as the referee blew the final whistle?

'At last,' yawned Sarah. 'Can we go home now? I have toenails to paint.'

'Wait!' Kate grabbed her arm and tugged her back. 'I think Conrad's coming over.'

He was jogging towards them across the pitch, his shirt sticking to his skin, soaked through with sweat.

'PJ doesn't know what she's missing,' gasped Kate, gripping Sarah's hand. 'Take a look at that torso.'

He stopped before them, shaking his hair like a wet dog at the beach.

'Hey, girls. Did you enjoy the game?'

Sarah nodded. 'The best I've ever seen.' It wasn't exactly a lie. It was the only match she'd ever seen. 'That was a great goal.'

'They ought to make you man of the match,' Kate patted his arm. Any excuse to touch his pecs.

'Well, if you ever want to sketch a sporting legend,' he turned to Sarah smiling, 'I can make myself available.'

Sarah choked back a laugh. Who did he think he was? Did he actually believe that kicking a stupid ball around a field made him an interesting person? How could PJ go out with such an idiot?

'Sorry, I don't draw footballers,' she said. Besides, he'd never get his fat head through the Art room door.

'So what have you done with PJ?' He looked concerned for a second, then shook it off, putting an arm around both of them.

'Never mind, two gorgeous girls on the touchline are better than one.'

Flirting was Conrad's favourite pastime. He was doing it now. Staring at them with his big brown eyes, talking in a breathless, husky voice. 'Catch you later, maybe?' He gave them a quick squeeze, then ran off towards the changing rooms.

'Did you get a whiff of his armpits?' Sarah gasped. 'Hasn't he heard of soap?'

Kate linked arms with her laughing 'Give the poor guy a break. Football's a sweaty sport. He's not that bad.'

'No?' said Sarah thoughtfully. 'So why isn't PJ here?'

There could be a hundred different reasons why she hadn't shown up. Asking PJ 'why?' was like guessing the size of an iceberg. Only the iceberg really knew for sure . . .

Your Cheatin' Heart

'What's that supposed to be?' Sarah picked up Kate's scribbled picture and held it to the light. 'It looks like my art tutor, before the plastic surgery.'

'Good guess,' Kate grinned. 'But actually, it's a portrait of you.' She ducked swiftly. Sarah's hand missed her head by a millimetre.

'My nose isn't that big,' Sarah shrieked, ripping it up into tiny pieces.

Kate pretended to sulk. 'What did you do that for? I was going to pin it up in the coffee bar.'

'If you even attempt it, our friendship is over,' laughed Sarah, threatening her with a wet paint brush. 'Now do you want to see the new poster for the band, or not?'

She pulled it carefully out of her portfolio. The Judas Tree logo was in green and speckled gold, with shadowy, metallic-looking silhouettes of the band in the background. 'So what do you think?'

'Sarah!' Kate gasped impressed. 'It's brilliant.'

'I know, it should be hanging in a gallery next

♥ 44 ♥

to the *Mona Lisa*.' She tied back her hair and checked her watch. 'I thought you were meeting PJ?'

Kate shrugged. 'I haven't seen her all day.'

'Me neither. I wonder what she's up to?' Sarah sighed.

PJ was driving them both crazy. She was being unpredictable, evasive, and even more secretive than usual. She'd given them some feeble excuse about missing the football match because of a Business Studies project. A highly unlikely story, thought Sarah, putting the Judes poster carefully back in her portfolio.

Why couldn't she just tell them the truth for once, and put them out of their misery?

'Anyway, I haven't got time to talk about PJ now.' Kate grabbed her bag and had a final wander round the Art room. 'I've got an English essay to do.'

Kate was the gossip queen of college. Unless you counted big-mouth Mish, but she was bitchy about everyone. Kate wouldn't bitch about a friend. But she'd never abandon a juicy discussion on PJ's personal life either – unless she was planning a hot date. Or a spending spree.

Sarah flicked a piece of paper at her, teasing, 'What's the real reason you're deserting me?'

'I've already told you, I've got course work,' said Kate, a little too casually.

'Kate,' Sarah laughed, 'it's written all over your face.'

'What is?'

'Excitement. Since when did English make you glow?'

'That's sunburn, idiot,' Kate said glancing at her face in the window. 'I have to go.' And she made a quick exit, before Sarah got too close to the truth.

She skipped past the bus stop and across the green to the car park. Where Mark was waiting in his convertible, head back, shades on, soaking up the sun. Almost too peaceful to disturb, Kate thought, adjusting her bra for maximum lift.

'I was going to let you give me a ride home.' She rested her elbows on the door, flirting like a maniac. 'But I can see you're really busy.'

He grinned and patted the seat beside him. 'Get in, before I change my mind and make you walk.'

'Walking might be quicker.' She climbed over the jammed door, giggling. 'You should convert this heap of junk to petrol before the elastic band snaps.'

It was the third lift he'd given her this week. They left college at the same time most days. If she timed it right.

What else was she supposed to do for fun? PJ was busy being mysterious. Sarah virtually lived in the Art room. And things with Joe had finally fizzled out, with no bad feelings on either side. She suspected Joe was quite relieved.

Mark must have guessed the big romance was over. She'd spent enough time with him lately. In fact, as far as Kate could tell, he never actually went to any lessons.

She was glad. Mark was brilliant company. And those gorgeous green eyes. He had the longest lashes she'd ever seen on a lad . . .

'Who put the smile on your face?' Mark suddenly said, backing out of the car park. 'You can tell me, I'm good at keeping secrets, remember?'

He was talking about their cosy little rendez-vous in the boys' toilets. He hadn't even told Sarah about that. Thank God.

Kate let her long hair loose in the breeze, avoiding his eyes. 'Sorry to disappoint you, but I was just thinking about an essay.'

The truth was too hot to handle. She'd been day-dreaming about a kiss with Mark. A slow, passionate tongue curler, complete with romantic background music and a sunset.

She'd have to be more careful. As Sarah said, it was written all over her face. For days now, she'd been fighting it. The feeling that Mark was the most amazing guy she'd ever met. How come she'd never noticed it before? He was wild, funny, insanely sexy. Everything she'd ever wanted in a guy, and more. They had an explosive chemistry between them. She knew he could feel it too. It was as if he'd packed his bags and moved into her heart.

It was a very tempting idea, to let their friendship drift into something physical. There was just one tiny fly in the whole love and romance ointment. Sarah. Kate's best mate. Mark's girlfriend.

Forget the bargepole, if Kate so much as touched him with a toothpick, Sarah would kill them both. She might be arty and sensitive, but underneath, she had the temper of a maniac! She had to put an end to the flirting before she and Mark did something they'd both regret. Forever.

The lifts home from college had to stop. And from now on, she'd have to share her mid-morning muffins with someone safer. Kate sighed heavily. Life could be so cruel.

'So are you going to invite me in for a coffee?' Mark asked as they pulled up outside Kate's house. 'It's OK, I'm fully house trained.'

Kate couldn't help laughing. He looked so cute when he begged. And just one little coffee. What harm could that do? After today, she'd be staying out of his way anyway.

'Ten minutes,' she grinned. 'Then you have to leave.'

It was too risky to let him stay any longer. If Sarah came round on her way home from college and found Mark sitting in her kitchen, things could get messy.

Mark rummaged through the kitchen cupboards while she made the coffee.

'Hey, chocolate raisins,' he said, suddenly appearing beside her with a big box. 'I could get addicted to these, no problem.'

'I can't watch TV without them,' grinned Kate.

Mark chucked one up in the air and caught it in his mouth. 'See, you understand about chocolate raisins. With Sarah, nothing's simple. Everything has to be so deep and meaningful. Sometimes, I just can't figure her out . . .'

'Don't worry,' Kate, grinned handing him a coffee. 'None of us can.'

He shook his head, sheepishly. 'Sorry, I forgot, Sarah's your mate. I shouldn't be telling you this stuff.'

Maybe not, but Kate was glad he had. It confirmed what she already thought. Mark and Sarah were not a match made in heaven. But Sarah was obviously smitten. So what could she do?

He followed her into the garden and sprawled out on the grass. Kate produced a packet of chocolate biscuits. She was about to make him an offer he couldn't refuse.

'These are all yours if,' she held them out of reach, 'you let me play your bass.'

She'd been pestering him for days to let her have a go.

'It's a deal.' He handed her his guitar. 'Wait, you're holding it all wrong.'

He showed her how to sit properly, then lay back in the grass, stuffing a whole biscuit into his mouth.

'Well, what do I do now?' asked Kate.

'Just play,' spluttered Mark, spraying her jeans with crumbs.

She plucked the strings with her fingers. It didn't sound very musical.

'Show me what I'm doing wrong,' she giggled.

He knelt behind her, putting his arms around her shoulders, moving her fingers into place. His fringe tickled her skin as he leant forward.

Kate held her breath. If he got any closer, she'd melt into a puddle of drool.

'You have to be more firm,' he said, tucking her hair behind her ear, his face resting gently against her cheek. It felt like heaven. So soft and smooth her legs turned instantly to blancmange.

She tried desperately to think of Sarah. The mate she'd known since high school. Her best friend in the whole world.

It was impossible. She couldn't think straight when Mark was so close. He scrambled her loyalties like fluffy egg whites.

'I didn't know playing the bass could be so cosy,' she said in a flirty whisper.

He brushed her hand with his fingers, and she could feel him smiling.

If she just tilted her chin upwards, she'd be in perfect snogging position . . .

She pulled away from him suddenly, handing back his bass in a fluster. 'You're coffee's getting cold,' she gasped.

Mark stood up, running a hand through his messy hair. 'I think I'd better go.'

Kate nodded.

'Thanks for the biscuits.' He gave her a quick mischievous grin, staring straight into her eyes. 'See you tomorrow.'

Kate watched him disappear round the front of the house, then collapsed in a heap on the grass, listening to him drive away.

They'd been dangerously close to a passionate snog. They could never, ever get that cosy again. From tomorrow, Mark was out of bounds – permanently.

'Kate, wait!' Sarah grabbed her arm. 'I've been following you all the way up the corridor. You were in a world of your own.'

'Sorry,' Kate sighed.

Guilt was giving her insomnia. Since her close encounter with Mark the other day, she'd been counting more sheep at night than a Welsh hill farmer. 'I'm just tired, I guess,' she yawned.

'I can see that. You've got huge bags under

your eyes. Here,' Sarah produced a tube of concealer. 'Cover up quick, before you give someone nightmares.'

'Thanks.' Kate took it grumpily. She couldn't help being snappy. How could she act normally when she'd almost snogged Sarah's boyfriend?

The worst thing was that she knew it could happen again. She thought about Mark a million times a day. The baby curls on the back of his neck. The wicked gleam in his eyes. The way he strutted across the coffee bar when he knew she was looking.

He might be out of bounds, but he was still playing havoc with her hormones. It had to stop. How could she risk losing Sarah – the friend who'd taught her how to pluck her eyebrows straight? Bonds like that could not be broken over a guy. Not even Mark.

She followed Sarah into the coffee bar with a heavy sigh. PJ was already there, surrounded by books and notes, finishing an essay.

'Hey, stranger,' Sarah grinned, sitting next to her. 'Where have you been hiding? We've missed you.'

'Really?' PJ sighed. 'Sorry. It's this stupid Business Studies project.'

'Yeah, right,' Sarah muttered under her breath, moving up to make room for Kate. 'Do we look like we believe in fairy tales? Why don't we have another girls' night in? You can tell us what you've really been doing.'

Since the other week round at PJ's, none of them had been making much time for the other two.

'Maybe next week,' Kate mumbled.

PJ had stopped working and was staring at her, concerned. 'Kate, you look terrible. What on earth have you been up to?'

'She's been in a total daze all day,' explained Sarah.

Kate picked up her purse and escaped to the coffee bar. 'I'll be fine when I've had some caffeine. Just stop fussing, OK?'

She couldn't face an interrogation. If they knew the real reason why she was in such a foul mood . . .

Mish was hovering by the table when she returned with an extra large cappuccino. Kate sighed. Could the day get any worse? Mish was like a blackhead – easy to squeeze, but she always came back.

'So the Judes are playing another gig?' she was saying to Sarah. 'I hope it's better than the last one. They sounded like a bunch of cats wailing.'

'That's because you were putting them off,' Kate interrupted. 'If you're going this time, could you please wear make-up?'

Mish turned on her with an acid smile. 'You know, you'd be a much nicer person if you took a vow of silence.'

'If you promise to transfer to another college, I might consider it.' Kate slammed her coffee down on the table, spilling it over PJ's books.

'Kate, watch what you're doing,' PJ snapped, rescuing her papers.

'I'm sorry.' Kate mopped up the mess with a tissue then sat back and sulked into her cappuccino. 'It was an accident, all right?'

'What's with you?' Sarah shuffled up close and put an arm around her shoulders.

Kate shrugged her off. Why did Sarah have to be so nice? It was like torture.

'Maybe you should just go home and get some sleep,' she suggested.

'Yeah,' PJ grinned. 'And wake up tomorrow in a better mood.'

A familiar voice interrupted, 'I can give you a lift if you want to go now?'

Suddenly, Mark was standing beside them, grinning at Kate, right under Sarah's nose. How could he? After the other day, he should be hiding his face under a paper bag.

'Don't let Kate scare you,' Sarah jumped up and kissed him swiftly. 'Her bark's worse than her bite. I'll meet you later, after rehearsals?'

'Wait for me. I've got to go and meet Conrad.'

PJ scooped up her folders, giving Kate a smile. 'I'll ring you later.'

Mark watched them both disappear into the corridor with an amused smile. 'Was it something I said?'

Kate wasn't in the mood for jokes. Especially as this was all Mark's fault anyway. If he wasn't so gorgeous and irresistible, she wouldn't be in this mess.

'I've got my guitar outside in the car,' he said, fiddling with his chunky silver ring. 'If you supply the coffee and chocolate raisins, I could give you another lesson?'

'Sorry.' Kate shook her head. 'The café's closed.'

Mark looked confused. 'Does that mean you don't want a lift?'

Was he stupid? They both knew where it would lead – straight into her back garden for a cosy snogging session. It was totally out of the question.

'Thanks for offering.' She pulled on her jacket, backing away from him towards the door. 'But I prefer the bus.'

Kate opened the fridge, grabbed the chocolate spread, a packet of muffins, two bananas, and a tub of ice cream from the freezer box. Late-night snacking helped her think.

She couldn't sleep anyway. The house was too

quiet. Every time she closed her eyes she saw Mark's face.

If only she'd met him before Joe. She'd never noticed how sexy Mark was until the incident in the boys' toilets. And since then, she'd been having wild, romantic dreams about him every night. They always ended in the same way. With a kiss. And if he was in her dreams, who, Kate wondered, was in his?

She was standing on a stool, searching for the chocolate sprinkles when she heard it. A gentle tapping on the kitchen window.

Kate froze. There it was again. Someone, or something, was trying to grab her attention. She crept across the kitchen floor, lifted the blind an inch, and peeped cautiously outside.

'Mark?' she gasped, letting it drop back again. What was he doing outside her kitchen window at this time of night?

Kate found the hand mirror her mum kept in the cupboard and inspected her face in a panic. It was worse than she'd feared – the massive spot she'd been prodding had taken over her whole chin. She turned out the light quickly, hoping it wouldn't glow in the dark.

She unlocked the door and yanked him inside. 'Quickly,' she hissed, 'before you wake up my parents.'

He looked amazing, with his wind-blown hair

tumbling across his face and his soft leather jacket hugging him tightly. Lucky leather jacket, Kate sighed. She knew it was wrong, but she was glad he'd come round to see her.

'Food,' he grinned, picking up the plate of muffins. 'Have you got any fudge sauce to go with these?'

'Never mind the sauce, you'll get me into trouble,' she whispered, grabbing the plate. 'It's almost midnight, Mark.'

'I know. I wanted to see what you wore in bed.' He looked her over with a cheeky smile. She even looked gorgeous in a scruffy T-shirt and cotton shorts. 'The bed socks are very cute, by the way,' he grinned.

'Idiot!' She hit his arm, trying to hide her feet. 'What do you want? Shhh . . .'

She put her hand over his warm mouth. Somebody was moving about upstairs. If her parents caught her with Mark, they'd stop her allowance. Life wouldn't be worth living.

She heard the toilet flushing and a door clicking shut. 'You have to leave, now,' she whispered urgently.

He wouldn't budge. 'Not until we sort his out, Kate.' He put his hands in his pockets, then took them out again, fidgeting nervously. 'You were angry with me in the coffee bar earlier. Because of the other day in the garden, right?'

♥ 57 ♥

'What's there to be mad about?' Kate shrugged. 'Nothing happened.'

'Only because you stopped it.'

He moved closer, pressing her into a corner. This wasn't exactly going according to plan. He'd come round to talk to Kate, not to make things ten times worse. But somehow, his hands were slipping round her waist, holding her close. And her hair smelt so wonderful, like oranges and warm sunshine.

'We can't do this,' Kate whispered. 'What about Sarah?' He didn't answer. Instead he kissed her gently. But it was more than just a snog. It made her whole body tingle.

'I wanted to kiss you in the garden,' he said softly, stroking her hair.

Kate nodded. 'Me too.'

She put her hands inside his warm leather jacket, tight around his waist, and kissed him right back.

♥

Oh Oh You're In Trouble

'I was starting to think you'd gone off me already,' Mark grinned, as Kate scrambled into the car, twenty minutes late. 'Or changed your mind about us.'

Kate sighed. 'Blame it on my English tutor. He wouldn't stop going on about Shakespeare. I mean, who cares about his stupid sonnets anyway?'

'Isn't Shakespeare supposed to be kind of romantic?' Mark said.

'If you're a crusty old teacher, maybe.' Kate dropped her bag on the floor, checked her hair in the rear view mirror, and smiled mischievously at Mark. 'So are you going to kiss me or what?'

Mark leant over and brushed her lips gently.

'Call that a kiss?' She grabbed his jacket lapels and pulled him closer. 'Come back over here, gorgeous, and do that again properly. We're not going anywhere until you get it right.'

'I was hoping you'd say that,' Mark grinned.

Kate demanded total snog satisfaction with every kiss. Sarah always held something back. Kate was much more fun. She just dived straight in and grabbed a piece of lip. She was amazing. He was suffering from snog exhaustion.

'How was that?' he gasped, breaking away from her breathless.

'Not bad, for a beginner.' She curled his hair round her finger, and tugged it gently. 'Come round to my house tomorrow night, and I'll show you my top snogging tips.'

Mark laughed. 'Sounds like fun.'

'It had better be.' Kate fastened her seat-belt. 'Let's get out of here before somebody sees us.'

It was a week since their first amazing kiss in her kitchen. And things had developed in a big way. She'd been meeting him in secret every day. In college, between lessons, after band rehearsals.

OK, so officially he was still Sarah's boyfriend. But it just felt so right. They both wanted more than friendship – a lot more. It was too late to stop it now.

Mark wasn't just renting a room in her heart any more. He'd taken possession of her whole being. Like a powerful love virus.

Kate got butterflies every time he even looked in her direction. His perfect kissable mouth, long dark lashes and wicked green eyes.

Mark felt the same way. He'd never actually said it, but he couldn't keep his hands off her. Any excuse to touch her hair or stroke her face. It was as if they were addicted to each other.

'So are you coming to the gig at the Warehouse next Saturday night?' said Mark, as they drove out of town. 'It's going to be the gig of the year. We've been working really hard, ironed out a few rough edges . . .'

'You mean you can sing in tune now?'

Mark grinned. 'Not yet. But I've still got a week to practise.'

Kate was desperate to see Mark on stage, all hot and sweaty, in his tight Judes T-shirt. She'd been dreaming about it all week. And the Warehouse was the best gig venue in town. Everyone from college had tickets. Including Sarah.

'What are you going to do?' Kate sighed. 'Dedicate a song to both of us?'

Mark shrugged. 'We'll just have to be extra careful.'

'And what if I get a passion attack?' Kate teased. 'I might lose control of my lips and snog you on stage.'

Mark glanced at her sideways to see if she was serious. 'Sarah might get just a teeny bit suspicious.'

So what was she supposed to do? Stay at home and watch TV, while everyone else had a great time at the gig? But if she went to the Warehouse, and Sarah found out about Mark . . .

Sarah still talked about him constantly. Gabbing on about the Judes, the gig, the future. Behaving as if she was destined to be the bass player's girlfriend forever. It was awful. Kate felt like a criminal, desperate and on the run from the Love Police. What was she going to do?

Suddenly she noticed that they were driving way out of town.

'Where are you taking me?' she asked, puzzled.

'To the beach.'

'Are you crazy?' Kate yelled above the noise of the car. 'It's Friday evening. It'll be swarming with people from college.'

Mark squeezed her knee. 'Relax. There's more than one beach.'

He drove for ages along the coast road. Finally he pulled over by a tiny, sandy cove, hidden from the road by grassy dunes. Kate had never seen it before.

'Privacy guaranteed,' Mark smiled, switching off the engine. 'You can take off that disguise now. Nobody's going to spot us here.'

Kate thumped him on the chest. 'I'm not wearing one, idiot.' The beach was totally deserted except for a couple of seagulls.

'It's so quiet,' she murmured.

'Yeah, too quiet.' Mark pulled off his trainers and chucked them over his head onto the back seat. 'I'll race you. Last one to the sea has to spend a day with Mish, and pretend to be her friend.'

'You're on!' Kate yanked off her boots, jumped

out of the car and knocked him sideways over a grassy dune. He caught her up quickly, tugging on her shirt tails to slow her down.

'That's not fair!' Kate shrieked, trying to shake him off. He let go suddenly. She fell forwards onto her knees in the sand, laughing.

Mark collapsed beside her. 'I won,' he gasped, out of breath.

'No way. You cheated.' She kicked sand at him. '*I* won.'

He was like a big kid. Kate wasn't complaining. At least he knew how to have fun. Unlike some people she could mention.

He sat up suddenly, looking thoughtful, letting sand run through his fingers. 'This is ridiculous, Kate. Why don't we just tell Sarah?'

Kate almost choked. 'Because she'd kill us both. With her bare hands.'

'How do you know?'

'Trust me, I know. I've still got the scars from the last fight we had,' she joked.

'So what are we going to do?'

If Mark had been anybody else's guy, she'd have gone public, and claimed him in the name of love, with no regrets. But when her best mate's feelings were involved, when there was a serious risk that this would destroy their friendship forever, that was a totally different kettle of kippers.

For the first time in her life, Kate was way out

of her depth. She didn't know how to handle it. It was a scary feeling. She didn't like it. And she didn't want to lose Sarah or Mark. But how could she keep them both?

'Why don't I just dump her?' Mark suggested.

Kate shook her head. 'She'd still blame me.'

'Not if I told her I'd forced you to snog me.'

'Wouldn't work.' She nudged his knee with hers. 'She knows me too well.' One look at her face, and Sarah would know exactly what Kate's feelings were for Mark.

There was only one solution to the whole messy problem. Kate had to chose between them. Sarah: her loyal best friend and keeper of Kate's most embarrassing secrets ever. Or Mark: gorgeous bass player with love-loaded lips, and an amp plugged straight into her heart. It was an impossible choice. She couldn't do it.

Mark put an arm around her shoulders. 'Maybe we should stop seeing each other?' he said softly, 'I'd understand, if that's what you wanted to do.'

Kate stared at him in shock. 'Is that what you want?'

'I asked first.' He rocked her gently. 'So, do you?'

Kate shook her head, rolled over and pinned him down in the sand, kissing him firmly.

'I guess that answers my question.' Mark licked his lips. 'You taste all salty, like a mermaid.'

'How many mermaids have you kissed lately?'

Kate stood up and dragged him to his feet. 'Penalty for cheating,' she grinned. 'You have to give me a piggyback all the way round the cove.'

'And what if my legs give way?' he laughed, rolling up his jeans.

Kate stroked his face. 'Then you'll just have to crawl, won't you?'

'Kate?' PJ looked at her curiously. 'Why have you got all this sand in your boots?' She tipped a pile of fine grains onto the grass.

'How did that get in there?' Kate tried to look amazed. She'd forgotten to empty them out over the weekend, after her trip to the beach with Mark. 'It must be from the other week,' she lied. 'You know, when we all went to the beach. Together. The six of us.'

'I guess so,' PJ nodded. She let the subject drop. But she could have sworn Kate had been wearing trainers that day, not boots.

She moved out of the sun, back under the shady trees. They were sitting on the college sports field, eating lunch in the sunshine for a change.

'What's in this sandwich?' Sarah said, holding it up to PJ.

'Salad and dolphin-friendly tuna. No mayo. Exactly what you asked me to get you.'

'Yeah, but this lettuce looks like it's already

been chewed.' Sarah pulled her sandwich apart, inspecting it carefully. 'Look,' she said, showing them both, 'teeth marks.'

'Yeah, right.' PJ laughed out loud. 'Why would anyone want to eat your sandwich?'

'Here, have mine instead. I'm not that hungry.' Kate swapped Sarah's dissected lunch for a cheese and tomato poppy seed roll.

She watched, amused, as Sarah brushed off the seeds. Sarah was such a one-off. Totally unique. When they were sitting outside like this in the sun, it was easy to block out the whole Mark situation and pretend it was happening to somebody else.

At least she'd stopped snapping at Sarah. It was scary how quickly you could learn to live with guilt.

'So guess what I heard about Mish?' Sarah sipped her coffee. 'You're never going to believe what she's done this time.'

Kate and PJ turned to face her eagerly. 'What?' they said together. Sarah always had the juiciest gossip.

'You know Jamie?' she continued. 'The college cricket star.'

Kate tried to picture him. 'Tight bum, unfortunate hair cut, wouldn't go out with Mish if she won the lottery and offered him a million?'

'That's the one,' Sarah grinned. 'Only it turns out she's fancied him for ages. Last night, in that new club, she walked straight up to him and snogged him, right in front of his girlfriend.'

'Oh my God!' shrieked Kate.

'Sounds like something you'd do.' PJ nudged her.

Kate froze in a panic. 'What do you mean?' she gasped.

'You know exactly what I mean.'

PJ knew. Kate could see it in her face. She'd guessed about Mark and she was about to dump Kate right in it up to her ears.

'Let's face it, you're as bad as Mish,' PJ giggled. 'You're always grabbing lads for a quick snog.'

PJ was just kidding around! Kate flopped back in the grass and gazed up at the sky, relieved.

'I only snog guys when I'm sure they really want me to,' she forced a smile. 'Mish takes them by surprise so they can't escape.'

'So then what happened?' PJ turned back to Sarah. 'Did Jamie run out of the club screaming?'

Sarah leant in closer. 'This is the best part. Jamie's girlfriend was so mad, she poured some guy's beer over Mish's head, told the bouncers she was a trouble-maker and had her thrown out.'

'She's such an embarrassment,' PJ sighed. 'Remember last summer, when she snogged the basketball team captain, on court?'

'Mish is going round telling everyone she did it for a dare.' Sarah lay back with her head on her bag. 'Jamie says it was like the attack of the killer blancmange.'

'Gross,' shivered Kate. 'The college should issue a warning about Mish. She's probably puckering up right now, ready to snog her next victim.'

'She's got a thing about good-looking sporty lads,' Sarah yawned.

'In that case,' Kate chucked a mint at PJ, 'you'd better warn Conrad.'

PJ fiddled with the little plastic elephant round her wrist. 'No need, he'd probably enjoy it.'

Conrad was convinced the whole college fancied him anyway – mainly because they did. But it would serve him right if Mish attempted a surprise snog.

'It's 12.40.' Sarah sat up, shielding her face from the sun. 'Anyone want to swap classes? I've got boring Art History all afternoon.' She gazed around the sports field sighing, her eyes locking onto a familiar figure. 'Hey Kate, isn't that Joe?'

'Where?' Kate rolled over in a panic. It was too late. Sarah was already waving him over. She grabbed her sun-glasses and hid behind them guiltily.

Joe could totally blow her cover. PJ and Sarah still believed she was seeing him on a casual basis. Well, she had to tell them something, right? But what if Joe told them the truth, and they started asking awkward questions?

It was like sitting on a ticking bomb, waiting for it to explode. And when it did . . .

'We haven't seen you around much lately,' said Sarah, as Joe sat down on the grass next to Kate.

Sarah had been wrong about Joe. OK, so he didn't talk much. But there was more to him behind that floppy fringe than a pretty face and dandruff.

'Kate must have been keeping you busy,' she grinned.

'Kate?' Joe stared at his ex in surprise. She was making threatening faces at him. He swept his black hair away from his eyes. 'I don't see her much . . . in college.'

Kate breathed a sigh of relief. Her secret was safe. For now. He might be dull, but when it came to personal stuff, Joe's lips were tighter than a baboon's bum. She'd never be nasty about him again.

But Sarah wasn't finished with him yet. 'Are you coming to the gig on Saturday night?'

'He doesn't like the Judes,' Kate butted in.

Joe frowned. Kate was acting really weird. 'A guy can change his mind, can't he?' he shrugged. 'I mean, is it OK with you, if I change my mind?'

'Of course, why shouldn't it be?' Kate snapped. She had to get rid of him quickly, before the conversation got dangerously personal. 'Don't you have classes to go to or something?'

'No, but I can take a hint.' He stood up awkwardly.

'Kate, you're so horrible to him,' Sarah whispered as he walked away. 'He's a big improvement on your last boyfriend. At least Joe doesn't burp in your face.'

'He just bores people to death instead,' Kate muttered under her breath.

'Bring him on Saturday night.'

'We'll see.' Kate turned away from them. She'd rather share a tent with Mish on a two-week camping holiday than take Joe to the gig.

'So will you do my hair tonight?' PJ asked Sarah, studying the packet of henna she'd bought in town.

Sarah was good at stuff like that. She should be, she changed her hair colour often enough. Kate got bored half-way through. PJ wanted all-over colour, not a leopard-skin effect.

'OK.' Sarah checked the instructions on the back of the packet. 'We could have another girls' night in. What do you think?'

Kate tried to look disappointed. 'I can't. I promised to wax my mum's legs, and she's got like, carpet coverage.'

It was a lie. She was seeing Mark. But she couldn't exactly tell them the truth, and that she was planning an evening of solid snogging.

PJ stood up, brushing down her skirt. 'I'm going back inside. Anyone coming?'

'I suppose so,' sighed Sarah.

Kate yawned and stretched. 'I think I'll stay out here for a while, and do my English homework.'

'Here.' PJ chucked her a slab of dark chocolate. 'Chocolate boosts your thinking power. It's official. I read it in a magazine.'

'In that case, you'd better give me some too.' Sarah broke off a large chunk. 'I need all the help I can get in Art History.'

Kate slipped the chocolate into her bag. Since she'd started seeing Mark, she'd totally lost her appetite. She couldn't sleep, she was permanently tired. It was like having a stomach bug, not a boyfriend.

'So what shall I wear to the gig?' Sarah asked PJ, as they walked away from Kate, back towards college. 'My rock-chick trousers with my Judas Tree T-shirt, or my vest top?'

'Do you have to decide right now? The gig's not until Saturday.' PJ considered it carefully. 'Definitely the vest top. Everyone knows you're the bassist's girlfriend, right? So why prove it with a T-shirt?'

'I guess so . . .' Sarah frowned. 'It's funny, I thought I'd be more excited than this.'

The Judes were finally playing a gig. She had an exclusive backstage pass, access all areas. The whole college would be there, watching her every move, green to the gills with envy. So why wasn't she getting giddy?

'Is everything OK with Mark?' asked PJ.

Sarah nodded. 'Fine. He's just been so wrapped up in rehearsals that I've hardly seen him for weeks.' Maybe she'd feel more involved on the night of the actual gig.

'Hey, girls!' Conrad ran up behind them, perspiring heavily from a lunch-time workout.

Sarah edged away from him. If one speck of boy sweat hit her new jacket . . .

'What happened to you last night?' he said to PJ. 'I thought we had a date. I waited ages . . .'

'Sorry.' PJ shrugged. 'I guess I just forgot.'

'How could you forget?' Conrad stared at her in disbelief.

PJ wasn't like other girlfriends he'd had in the past. She could be really sweet one day, giving him loads of attention. Then the next, she'd be sort of distant, as if he'd done something wrong, only he wasn't sure what.

'So what about tonight?' he asked. 'Do you want to go for a pizza?'

'I can't. I'm already doing something with Sarah.'

Sarah nodded. 'Hair stuff. It could get pretty messy.'

Conrad rested his hands on his hip bones with a sigh. 'Fine. Well, just fit me in sometime, OK? When it's convenient.'

'Don't be so touchy,' PJ whispered, tickling his

arm gently. 'I'll call you later.' She walked towards the main building, giving him a big smile.

Sarah followed, giving him a wide birth, just in case he started shaking his sweaty hair.

'What's going on?' she hissed, tugging PJ's bag. 'Have you two fallen out?'

'No. I just don't want to see him every night. I've got other stuff to do.'

'Like what?'

'Just stuff,' giggled PJ, opening the main doors.

Sarah let her go through first, glancing back over her shoulder. Conrad was still watching. He gave her a flirty grin.

'Don't waste your time, moron,' she tutted, turning away quickly. Conrad might be the biggest flirt in college, but that didn't give him the right to try it on with everybody.

He'd been flirting with her a lot lately. It was getting on her nerves. What did he expect her to do? Blow him a big sloppy kiss in front of PJ?

She wasn't interested anyway. Conrad was way too sweaty and far too in love with himself to be remotely attractive.

'Poor PJ,' she muttered. Mark had his faults, but at least he didn't eye up other girls.

Kate bought a cappuccino and found a free seat in the coffee bar. She hated Friday afternoons.

Everyone else finished college early, and she still had two whole hours of boring English to sit through. It wasn't fair.

Mark was rehearsing with the Judes all afternoon, so a quick snog in the stationery cupboard was totally out of the question. Pity, Kate thought. She needed something to get her through another batch of Shakespeare's sonnets.

She got out her English folder, then closed it again instantly with a wicked smile. Mish had just walked into the coffee bar, alone. She'd been keeping a very low profile since the Jamie incident. Kate hadn't seen her all week. She picked up her drink and followed Mish across the room.

'Hey, you look fabulous today,' she grinned, sitting down at her table. 'No, honestly, I really mean it.'

Mish glowered at her suspiciously but said nothing.

'Your hair's in great condition,' Kate continued. 'Must be that new shampoo I hear you're using. What's it called again?' Kate suddenly snapped her fingers. 'Now I remember. Warm beer rinse in a night club.'

'Just drop dead,' scowled Mish, grabbing her folder and moving to another table.

Kate followed. Mish was such a bitch. Now it was her turn to suffer. She deserved everything she was about to get.

'What's the matter?' Kate teased. 'Lost your sense of humour all of a sudden?'

Mish hissed. 'Just get out of my face, OK?'

'What a coincidence.' Kate tapped her knee. 'I hear that's exactly what Jamie said after you'd vacuumed out his mouth.'

Mish glared at her, going an angry shade of red. For once in her life, she was speechless.

'So is it true you sucked out one of his fillings?' Kate was enjoying herself now. 'That's just so romantic,' she sighed sarcastically. 'You could put it on a chain and wear it round your neck as a token of your love.'

Mish leapt up in a rage. 'I did it as a dare, OK? Not that it's any of your business, you nosey cow.' She stormed across the room and out of the coffee bar.

'Jamie sends his love,' Kate yelled after her. She put her hands behind her head with a satisfied smile.

Giving Mish a shot of her own venom, now that was Kate's idea of community service.

'So I hear you dissed Mish this afternoon,' said Mark, peeping round Kate's kitchen door.

'She deserved it.' Kate dragged him inside to revive her snog-starved lips. A couple of hours without Mark, and she got withdrawal symptoms.

Dry lips, fuzzy brain, constant day-dreaming. How could one scruffy bass player give her so many palpitations?

She put her hands in his jacket pockets and kissed him.

'And what's this?' She pulled a box out of the lining. Inside it was a tiny heart shaped chocolate, with a big pink K in icing sugar on it. 'Is this for me?' she grinned.

Mark nodded and scratched his head looking embarrassed. 'I was going to give it to you . . . someday.'

When he'd plucked up the courage. He'd never bought anything heart-shaped for a girl before. Except his mum. And she didn't count.

It was totally bizarre. He'd driven into town for a new set of windscreen wipers, and come home with a chocolate instead. Kate was having a weird effect on his life.

'It's so cute,' she tickling his ribs. 'I love it.'

Mark reached past her into the cupboard for the chocolate raisins, hiding a smile. 'Well, aren't you going to eat it?'

'No way.' Was he crazy? She couldn't just scoff it down with a mug of coffee. It was special. She was going to keep it on her bedside table where she could look at it. But if he ever dumped her, she'd feed it to the dog, pronto.

'Sarah dropped by the attic this afternoon,' he

said. 'She wanted to know why I'm never at home when she phones.'

Kate bit her lip guiltily. They hadn't discussed Sarah much since the beach, last Friday.

Mark had been at rehearsals most evenings, and when he finally got to her house, they'd avoided the subject and just snogged instead – on the sofa, in the kitchen, by the front door for half an hour before he left. But all the time, Sarah was at the back of her mind. It was almost as if she was watching them. They couldn't keep pretending she didn't exist.

'Do you think she's getting suspicious?' asked Kate.

'Not yet.' Mark sat down and pulled Kate onto his knee. 'But we'll have to tell her soon.'

It was time she stopped burying her head in the sand, ostrich style, and faced up to reality. She couldn't give up Mark, and she hated lying to Sarah. She had to tell her the truth before somebody else did.

'I'll break it to her next week.' Kate fiddled anxiously with her pendant. 'After the gig.'

If she picked the right moment, when Sarah was in an understanding mood . . .

'Phone's ringing,' Mark whispered in her ear.

Kate got up with a heavy sigh to answer it. It was Sarah.

Mark followed her into the hall and put his arms round her waist, whispering, 'Who is it?'

'Who have you got in the hall with you?' asked Sarah curiously.

'Tell her now,' Mark hissed. 'There's no time like the present . . .'

Kate shook her head.

'Then let me do it.' He grabbed the phone. Kate prised it out of his fingers and pushed him away.

'Kate? Is that Joe's voice I can hear? No wonder you took so long answering the phone,' Sarah giggled. 'Did I catch you two in the middle of a snog?'

'Joe's not here. It's the TV,' she lied nervously. Mark was clamped around her waist again, nibbling at her ear. 'Ow!' she hissed.

'Kate, what's going on?' said Sarah. 'You sound like you're being mugged.'

'I'm OK. I've just been . . . bitten by something. Can you hang on for a second?'

She dragged Mark into the kitchen. 'Go and eat a biscuit if you're hungry, and leave my lobes alone.'

She ran back into the hall, flustered. If Sarah wasn't suspicious before, she'd be very curious by now. 'So what did you want to ask me?'

'Oh yeah. It's about tomorrow night.'

Kate held her breath. What now?

'I'm going shopping all day, so I'll just meet you at the gig, OK?'

Perfect. Kate could go to the Warehouse, avoid

Sarah in the crowd and get to see Mark on stage. 'No problem,' she said, relieved.

'I've got to go. Dad's taking us all out for a Chinese meal. He orders like sixteen courses. It takes all night. So don't even try to phone me,' she yawned. 'I'll be out until late. See you tomorrow.'

Kate hung up quickly. The last thing she wanted to do was speak to Sarah again while Mark was in the house.

'Is it safe to come out now?' he grinned, wandering back into the hall.

'She could have recognised your voice, stupid.' Kate flicked his ear.

'But she didn't.' He grabbed hold of her suddenly and swung her round. 'Let's go for a pizza,' he whispered in her ear. 'Then we can run through your snogging tips again. I didn't quite get the hang of some of the technical stuff last time.'

Any excuse for a snog. Still, there was no point letting one phone call ruin the whole evening.

'What are we waiting for?' Kate giggled. There'd be plenty of time to feel guilty about Sarah again tomorrow.

The pizza place was on the outskirts of town. Kate ran in, picked up their order – deep-pan pepperoni with extra cheese and mushrooms – then dived back into the car.

'Um, smells delicious.' Mark sniffed the box hungrily, turning the car around. 'Can we eat it now? I'm starving.'

Kate flicked the top open and shoved a large slice into his mouth.

'Ow! It's hot,' he gasped, blowing out steam to cool it down. 'Give me more,' he grinned, mouth wide open, waiting for another bite of crispy crust.

'Pig,' Kate giggled. 'Who bought this pizza anyway?'

'You did,' he whimpered hungrily, as she hugged the box and took a big bite of melted cheese and mushroom. 'You can't eat a whole pizza by yourself.'

'Just watch me,' Kate teased, grabbing another slice, wafting it under his nose, then lining it up with her mouth. 'OK, you can have another bit,' she paused at the last second, 'if you tell me I'm the most gorgeous girl you've ever been out with in your life.'

Mark made a lunge for the pizza and sank his teeth in.

'Hey!' Kate yelled. 'That's cheating.'

Mark munched happily as they stopped at a set of traffic lights. He leant forward to fiddle with the car radio. 'What do you want? Dance chart, or indie?'

'Whatever.' Kate rested her arm round his

shoulders, and licked her pepperoni-flavoured fingers. The skin on the back of his neck was baby soft, with one cute little curl growing up instead of down. She stroked his neck lazily, gazing out of the car window.

Her fingers suddenly froze. Standing on the pavement opposite, staring right back in at her, was a girl who looked suspiciously like – it couldn't be – Mish?

'Oh my God!' Kate gasped, sliding down in her seat so fast that her knees hit the floor with a thud. It was Mish all right. Nobody else had that same sickly smile.

'What's wrong with you?' Mark laughed. 'If my driving scares you that much . . .'

'Turn around and look out the window,' she hissed. 'Who do you see?'

Mark peered out the window. 'What am I supposed to see . . . Mish!'

So it was true. She wasn't hallucinating. 'Is she looking? Can she see me?' Kate hissed in a panic.

Mark turned up the collar on his jacket to hide his face, and sank low in his seat. 'She can see us both. She's waving at me. What do I do? Wave back? Oh no, I don't believe it . . .'

'What now?' Kate moaned.

'She's crossing the road, right in front of the car.'

'The bitch!'

Kate squashed herself under the dashboard, kneeling in the soggy pizza. It was useless trying to hide anyway. Mish was now standing on the pavement, right outside the passenger door, peering in at her.

The lights turned to green at last. 'Just get me out of here.' Kate scrambled back into her seat. What was the point of hiding? Mish had seen everything. The cosy pizza for two, Kate stroking Mark's neck. Kate looking guilty, trying to hide.

'Will she tell Sarah?' Mark asked anxiously.

'What do you think?' Kate peeled a slice of pepperoni off her jeans, and glanced back over her shoulder. Mish was still watching.

'We're in big, big trouble,' she sighed.

It was payback time. Mish had all the ammunition she needed to ruin Kate's life. And she wouldn't be afraid to use it.

♥

Fess Up

Kate got out of the taxi, put on her shades and strutted straight to the front of the long queue, outside the Warehouse. 'It's OK, I'm not pushing in,' she said, flicking her hair in the doorman's face. 'I'm on the guest list.'

She ducked past him quickly before he could check. She wasn't even sure there was a guest list. She just had to get inside, find Sarah and come clean. Confess everything. Tell her the whole sordid story, face to face. Before blabber-mouth Mish beat her to it.

And Mish *would* tell – she'd enjoy every second of it. She'd love to get her revenge for all the times Kate had given her a real grilling, especially over Jamie. She'd probably tell Sarah that Kate and Mark were snogging up a storm, holding up traffic. Kate cringed at the thought. She had to stop it from happening.

She raced down the stairs into the gig room and bumped into PJ coming the other way.

'Am I glad to see you,' she sighed with relief.

PJ was brilliant in a crisis. She kept her cool, gave great advice. If only Kate could tell her about Mark . . .

'It's mad in there,' yelled PJ, pulling on her jacket. 'Don't go in without earplugs.' She stared at Kate strangely. 'What happened to your hair?'

Kate's hair was usually perfect. But today . . . God, she looked as though she'd been through a sheep-dip.

'Is it really bad?' Kate frowned.

'That depends,' PJ cringed. 'How bad do you think it is?'

'It's that stupid hot oil stuff.' Kate shoved a handful of grips at her, and dragged PJ into a quiet corner to try to repair the damage. 'They should put a warning on the packet,' she fumed, piling her hair on top of her head. 'Nobody told me about the fluffy side effects.'

Why did everything have to go wrong on the same day? 'Is that the Judes I can hear on stage?' she shouted, tidying up the loose ends.

PJ shook her head. 'It's some stupid DJ. The bands are on later. They've got three playing tonight. The Judes are on second . . .'

PJ stopped talking. Kate wasn't listening to a word she said. She was too busy scanning the room behind her, looking for someone.

'Just stop me if I'm boring you,' she grinned.

'I'm sorry,' Kate groaned. 'It's not you. I've had a lousy day.'

That was the understatement of the year. It had been the worst twenty-four hours of her entire life, starting last night, when Mish had caught her canoodling with Mark in his convertible. She'd been wide awake for hours, restless and guilty, desperate to talk to Sarah to try to sort things out. But she couldn't. Sarah wasn't in.

When she'd finally fallen asleep, she'd had a nightmare. She was in an English lesson, only it was in an old theatre and Mish was taking the class, with her teaching assistant – William Shakespeare. They made Kate stand up and tell everyone how she'd cheated on her best friend. It was totally humiliating. But she couldn't escape because her feet were tied together. And then Sarah appeared, in Mark's car, and tried to run her over.

She'd woken up late the next morning in a cold sweat, clutching her pillow. She'd raced round to Sarah's to catch her before she went shopping. But she was too late. Sarah had already gone.

Kate had left her a message, saying, 'Phone me. URGENT', in huge black letters, underlined about twenty times.

She'd spent the rest of the day waiting for the phone to ring, getting totally paranoid. By six o'clock, Sarah still wasn't back from town. How long did it take to buy one stupid pair of boots anyway?

And why hadn't Mark phoned her since last

night? Maybe he'd decided that being with Kate was too much trouble. That Sarah was the girl for him after all. He'd been a little too concerned about her after the incident with Mish, saying, 'Sarah's going to be really upset' and 'I wish we didn't have to hurt her'.

Kate didn't want to hurt her either. But why was Mark suddenly so worried? Maybe he'd met her in town and they'd patched things up?

Sarah still fancied Mark. Why else would she talk about him and the Judes all the time? Why else would she ignore Kate's note?

She still hadn't heard from either of them by the time she went to the gig. At least PJ was here. Good, reliable, dependable PJ. Kate gave her arm a squeeze.

'Actually I'm just leaving,' PJ shouted over the noise of the band.

Kate gripped her wrists in a panic. 'You can't. You promised you'd come to the gig.'

PJ shook herself free. 'I didn't say I'd stay all night.'

'But it's only eight thirty.'

'Sorry,' shrugged PJ. 'I've already made other arrangements. I can't cancel now.'

What arrangements? With whom? She couldn't just walk out on the gig of the year before it had even started. People were fighting to get in.

'What kind of a friend are you?' Kate scowled.

'Friends are supposed to be there for each other. You can't just desert me. You have to stay.'

'Why?' yelled PJ. 'Are you in trouble?'

It wouldn't be the first time. Kate was like a trouble-seeking missile. She loved being the centre of attention. And PJ recognised the danger signs: the bad mood, the yelling, the jumpy way she was acting. It all added up to trouble.

'What have you done?' she shouted.

'Why does everyone always assume I'm in trouble?' OK, so it was true, this time, but that was beside the point. 'Anyway, I can't talk about it,' she sighed miserably.

PJ frowned. 'It can't be that bad.'

Bad wasn't the word. More like the biggest disaster of the century. 'Is Sarah here?' she asked. The least PJ could do was give Kate some vital information before she completely deserted her.

'She's around somewhere. I lost her by the pool room.'

'Is she OK?' asked Kate. 'I mean, she's not acting strangely or anything?'

'No more than usual,' grinned PJ.

'Have you seen anyone else?'

'God, what is this, the Spanish Inquisition?' PJ thought for a second. 'Shelley's here, and Sarah's arty mates. Just the usual crowd.'

'What about Mish?'

PJ tutted. 'Unfortunately. She cornered me in the

♥ 87 ♥

toilets. Told me I should grow my hair to cover up my huge ears.'

'Cheeky bitch,' grinned Kate. 'Don't listen to her. You've got really cute ears.'

Mish enjoyed being a cow. It was the only thing she was any good at.

PJ was checking her watch. 'If I don't go now, I'm going to be late.'

'For what?' Kate yelled. It was worth a try. But PJ pretended she hadn't heard and gave Kate a quick hug, adding 'Phone me tomorrow with all the gossip.'

There'd be plenty of it. Mark, Kate and Sarah, the whole messy love triangle exposed. Joe was partly to blame, of course. If he'd made more of an effort, tried a little bit harder to be interesting and sexy, she might never have fancied Mark.

PJ left Kate and battled her way towards the exit. Sarah was standing by the open door, looking flushed.

'It's so hot in there,' she said, fanning her face with her backstage pass.

PJ took hold of her arm and lead her to the top of the stairs. 'Kate's here,' she said, pointing to the empty corner where they'd just been talking. 'Well, she was a minute ago. She's acting really weird. I think she's in trouble.'

'She left me note,' said Sarah, puzzled, 'telling me to phone her urgently.' But Kate had already left for the gig by the time she'd got back from town. 'Do you think that's got something to do with it?'

'Who knows?' grinned PJ.

Kate was useless at keeping stuff to herself. Sooner or later – usually sooner – she just had to tell someone. Life was never dull with her around.

'So where's Conrad?' Sarah asked. She grabbed PJ's arm and inspected her wrist. 'Where's your charm bracelet? The one he gave you, with the little plastic elephant?'

'I took it off,' PJ said.

Sarah looked surprised. 'Does that mean that you two have broken up?'

'It means I didn't want to lose it. It's pretty rough down there.' PJ glanced back into the gig room. 'Conrad would be really hurt if I lost it. He can be quite sweet sometimes. What's up with you?'

Sarah was suddenly looking depressed.

'Oh, I get it.' PJ put an arm around her. 'You were hoping I'd finished with Conrad, so I'd finally dish the dirt on him, right?'

'Wrong,' Sarah mumbled under her breath. PJ didn't 'get it' at all.

'Well, sorry to disappoint you.' PJ buttoned up

her jacket, checked her watch, then headed for the door. 'I'd better be going. See you on Monday.'

'Monday.' Sarah waved, and gazed back down into the gig room with a massive sigh.

Kate wandered into the gig room. The Warehouse was the kind of place that looked better in the dark. It felt industrial, with massive iron girders everywhere and a strange smell of mouldy cheese. It was perfect for the Judes. In a place like this, they had nothing to live up to.

It was packed already. How was Kate supposed to find anyone? She scanned the room quickly. There was no sign of Sarah. Or Mish. But Shelley was dancing with some guys from college over by the pool room.

She battled her way around the edge of the floor and crashed straight into Joe by the bar.

'What are you doing here?' she tutted. He was always appearing in the wrong place at the wrong time. It was as if he did it on purpose, just to annoy her.

'It's nice to see you too,' he laughed, staring at her.

'What?' Kate snapped. 'Have I got dirt on my face or something?'

'No, it's your hair. You've done something different to it. It looks great.'

Typical. When they'd been an item and she'd spent hours styling it, he'd never even noticed. But today, when it looked worse than a bird's nest in a hurricane, he liked it. Sometimes lads were a total mystery. Particularly Joe.

Kate looked him over carefully. He was wearing a white shirt and worn jeans that made his legs look even longer and leaner than they already were. He had so much style. It was just a shame about the built-in snooze factor.

'So who are you here with?' she asked impatiently.

'The guys from college. But I'm just about to leave. I've had enough,' he grinned. 'Not my kind of music.'

'If you bump into Sarah, tell her I'm looking for her.'

Joe nodded.

Kate dived past him. She had more important things to do than try to prise Joe out of his shell.

She grabbed Shelley. 'Have you seen Sarah?' she yelled.

Shelley nodded. 'About ten minutes ago. You're the second person to ask me that. Mish was looking for her too.' Kate felt sick. What if she'd already told Sarah everything?

'If you see her again,' Kate shouted in Shelley's ear, 'tell her I need to speak to her, urgently.'

Shelley gave her the thumbs up. 'You could try the toilets. She was heading that way with a lipstick.'

'That figures.' Why didn't Kate think of that? Sarah was never far from a mirror.

She dashed round the side of the room, through a poky door, down two flights of steps and along a dark corridor. Why were the girls' toilets always miles away in places like this? The boys' room was right next to the main entrance. It wasn't fair.

Kate squeezed through the door. They were the worst toilets she'd ever seen. One cracked mirror. No ventilation. The air was thick with hairspray fog and perfume that smelt like carpet cleaner.

Sarah wasn't even there, unless she was hiding in a cubicle. Kate had to make sure.

She banged on the first door. There was no answer. She ducked down and checked for shoes under the gap. White stilettoes. Definitely not Sarah's. She wouldn't be caught dead in a pair of those.

The next cubicle – chunky ankle boots. Not Sarah's style. Kate knocked on cubicle three, shouting, 'Sarah? Are you in there?'

'I think I would have noticed if she was,' an unfamiliar voice said back.

'No need to be so touchy,' Kate muttered. At least she knew Sarah wasn't hiding from her.

She squeezed in front of the tiny mirror. She'd lost her mascara. Her face looked naked without it. She'd grabbed her mum's in a panic on the way out of the house. But now she wasn't sure it was safe to use. It looked disgustingly thick and lumpy when she inspected it under the lights. If she blinked before it dried, she'd tarmac her lashes together.

'Could you get your elbow out of my face?' she snapped at the girl beside her. 'I need to concentrate here, OK?' One false move and she'd be stuck with very unattractive panda eyes all night.

She fought her way back out of the cramped toilets. If Sarah wasn't fixing her face, there was only one place she could be: backstage with Mark. Sarah wouldn't miss out on all that pre-gig excitement. She'd be right in there, glued to his side, making sure everyone saw them together.

Kate walked around the other side of the stage and through the door marked private. You couldn't even call it a backstage area. It was just a long dingy corridor with a sink. Not exactly a luxury dressing room. Still, stuff like that didn't bother Mark. He was happy sitting on a crate, strumming his guitar. He looked so cute when he was concentrating.

Kate crept up behind him. But there was no sign of Sarah anywhere. So where the hell was she? It didn't make sense. She'd been going on about this gig for weeks. Why wasn't she backstage, lapping up the attention?

Still, Kate was relieved. At least it meant her Mark/Sarah reunion theory was totally wrong.

She put her arms around Mark's neck. 'Are you

♥ 93 ♥

OK?' she whispered. 'Did somebody steal your wallet?'

He looked at her puzzled. 'No, it's right here. Why?'

'Is there any money in it?'

He flicked it open and tipped the change into his hand.

'So you had money but you didn't bother to phone me? Well, thanks a lot,' she hissed, tightening her grip around him. 'I've been going crazy on my own all day. I even thought maybe you'd . . .'

'Maybe I'd what?' Mark made room for her on the crate and slipped a hand round her waist.

'Never mind,' she sighed, relieved. It sounded stupid now. Of course he hadn't gone back to Sarah. She'd just got totally paranoid, sitting at home, with nobody to talk to. What else was she supposed to think?

'The guys have been working me really hard,' he explained. 'Sorry, I just didn't get a chance . . .'

'Sorry isn't good enough,' Kate grinned. 'Make it up to me right now, or I'm turning you over to Mish and Sarah.'

Mark laughed. 'You wouldn't dare.' He cupped her face in his hands and kissed her. Twice.

'Not bad for a bass boy.' Kate nudged him playfully. 'But I want more, later . . . Have you seen Sarah?'

Mark rested his chin on her shoulder. 'She was here. Fifteen minutes ago. It was awful, Kate. I didn't know what to say to her.'

OK, so Mark loved girls. But he'd never actually been out with two at the same time before. It was far too complicated. He liked to keep things simple.

'Do you have to tell Sarah everything?' he sighed.

'If I don't, Mish will.'

'What are you going to say to her?' he asked.

'Don't know,' Kate shrugged. 'Whatever comes into my head at the time, I guess.' She just hoped it wasn't something totally stupid.

Mark put his arms around her and gave her a tight squeeze. 'Whatever happens, you've still got me.'

But she couldn't phone Mark up, mid-hair crisis, and ask to borrow his curling tongs. They couldn't try out make-up together, or giggle at the back of classes about boys. She was missing Sarah already and they hadn't even fallen out yet.

She was one mixed-up chick and it was a feeling she didn't like.

She patted Mark's knee. 'Are you nervous about the gig?'

Mark nodded. 'Either that or I've got indigestion.'

'I know a good cure for both.' Kate pulled him closer and kissed him.

She stopped suddenly.

'What's wrong?' Mark checked his breath in his cupped hand. 'I brushed my teeth like, twenty minutes ago, in case you stopped by.'

Kate ducked behind him. She'd just caught a glimpse of somebody with long auburn hair. 'Sarah!' she hissed.

'Where?' Mark looked round nervously, then burst out laughing.

'That's not Sarah,' he said, pulling her round in front of him. 'Look, it's Paul. The drummer. Hey, Paul!' he shouted over. 'Time to get your hair cut, mate. Kate thought you were a girl.'

It wasn't funny. What if it had been Sarah? What if Mish was sharing her little secret with her right now?

Kate had to find her. 'How am I going to tell her?' She buried her face in Mark's jacket.

Mark clasped her hand and led her round the corner to the fire escape steps, where they could talk in private. 'I've hardly seen Sarah for weeks.' And they hadn't even had a proper snog for ages. Just a quick brush of the lips. He'd managed to avoid swapping spit. 'She'll probably be glad to get rid of me,' he grinned.

'No,' Kate shook her head. 'She still likes you. You've just been too busy to notice.'

Mark stroked her hair and kissed her gently. He couldn't get enough of Kate. He'd even written a song about her. He hadn't plucked up the courage to play it to her yet. He was half-afraid she'd laugh. Kate wasn't easy to impress, but that was one of the things he loved about her.

'Hey, Romeo!' The Judes' lead singer was suddenly standing before them. 'In case you've forgotten, we're supposed to be playing a gig. So stop snogging and get your butt out here. We're on stage in two minutes.'

'Is he always so obnoxious?' Kate hissed as he walked away.

'He's usually worse,' Mark smiled. 'But he's a great front man for the band. So I guess we're stuck with him.'

Mark picked up his guitar. 'Are you coming out the front to watch?'

Kate sighed. 'I have to find Sarah.'

'If you wait until the gig's over, I'll come and help you. But if she starts throwing things, I want protection.'

'Coward!' Kate prodded him playfully. 'I can't wait that long.'

Mark looked relieved. It was probably better if she faced Sarah alone anyway. If she saw Kate and Mark together, it might make things worse.

'We're only on for twenty minutes. I'll come and find you after.' He winked at her and followed the rest of the band.

*

Kate slipped back into the gig room as the Judes stepped out onto the stage. The obnoxious lead singer was leaping about like a maniac, trying to eat the microphone. With a mouth like his, he could fit it in sideways and still have room for a burger. At least the spooky green spot lights hid his zits.

They went straight into the first song. No introduction. Kate was shocked. The Judes could actually play in tune. But Mark was the star of the show. Definitely the cutest guy in the band. No contest. He was a natural, born to be a bassist.

Kate sighed. She could stand and drool over him all night, but time was running out. Mish was on a mission to wreck her life, and she had to be stopped.

She looked around the room in a panic. She'd never find Sarah now. The audience were going crazy, chanting, 'Judes! Judes! Judes!' and leaping about all over the place.

Shelley was standing a few feet away, waving her over. Maybe she'd found Sarah?

'Where is she?' yelled Kate, clinging onto her sleeve, in case they got separated in the crush.

'I've been asking around. Nobody's seen her for ages.'

'Tell me something I don't know,' frowned Kate.

It was almost as if Sarah was avoiding her. If Mish had spilt the beans she wouldn't be hiding. She'd be dragging Kate outside for a showdown.

'Maybe she's already gone home?' Shelley shouted.

Kate shook her head. 'She wouldn't just leave.' Not while the Judes were on stage. Why wasn't she standing somewhere obvious where everyone could see her? Why wasn't she watching Mark? Wasn't that what girlfriends were supposed to do?

There was a sudden cheer from the audience. Kate turned to see what was happening. Mark had stripped off his Judas Tree T-shirt and was swinging it round his head. And across his bare chest, in black marker pen, he'd written 'SEXY'.

Kate couldn't help grinning. He was such a show-off. He'd do anything for a laugh. He threw his T-shirt into the crowd and took a bow.

'This one's new,' he said, breathless, into the microphone. Kate recognised the beginning of 'Aliens Shop at Spaceways', her favourite Judes song. She desperately wanted to stand and watch him sing it. She loved the way his lips curled up at the edges when he hit the high notes – if he hit the high notes! But she had to think quickly.

Sarah sometimes liked to stand up in the gallery with her arty mates. Kate pushed through the crowd and ran up the steps. There was no sign of her. She peered over the railings and down into the gig room. Suddenly, Sarah was there, standing right over on the other side, where Kate had just been talking to Shelley.

She wasn't the only person to spot Sarah. Mish was already trying to reach her. And she had a good head start. If Kate could just stop her . . .

She dived down the stairs, tripping over a first-year art student. 'Get out of my way, idiot,' she screamed, jumping over her legs, and barging her way through the audience. She found Mish standing alone. Sarah had disappeared again.

Kate took Mish by the elbows and spun her round, yelling, 'This is between me and Sarah. It's got nothing to do with you. So keep your fat nose out of it, OK?'

Mish gave her a sarcastic smile. 'You should have thought of that before you stirred things up with Jamie.'

'That was different,' Kate shouted. 'You deserved it.'

'Oh, and I suppose you don't?' Mish taunted her.

'At least I don't embarrass myself in night clubs.'

'I can't wait to tell Sarah what I caught you doing with her boyfriend in his car.'

Mish was standing so close that she could see every sweaty pore on her hot skin. 'Go ahead and tell her,' Kate folded her arms. 'You'll have to find her first.'

'No problem!' Mish flung her out of the way. 'I know exactly where she is.'

'You're not going anywhere without me!' Kate grabbed her arm. Mish yanked it free and pushed into the audience. Kate dived after her, but Mish had already been swallowed up by the heaving crowd at the foot of the stage. From there, she could have gone anywhere: the toilets, backstage, the pool room, the gallery.

Kate turned around frantically, trying to catch a glimpse of her. But it was hopeless. Everyone looked the same under the spooky green lights.

She gave up. Mish – the malicious bitch – had finally won. And it was all Kate's fault. Why had she let Mark kiss her that night in the kitchen? If she'd just resisted temptation, sent him home and warned him never to call round again, like a good friend was supposed to, none of this would be happening.

But he'd been so close, so utterly kissable. Her lips had been out of control, puckering up before she could stop them.

She'd really messed up. Broken all the rules of friendship. Things with Sarah would never be the same again. There would be separate tables in the coffee bar, different bus routes home, awkward meetings around college.

Kate stomped towards the side exit. She needed some air. Some space to breath and get her head together. She couldn't think straight with a load of morons jumping about and singing badly out of tune down her ear. She pushed the door open, ran down the steps and leant against the wall outside. It felt deliciously cool.

A snogging couple were standing close by in the shadows, making disgusting slurping noises. Kate glared round at them, then did a double take.

The guy looked strangely familiar. Tall, athletic, short cropped hair. It had to be Conrad. Kate didn't even know he was at the gig. PJ must have changed her mind and come back to see him. The girl he was with – Kate couldn't see properly in the shadows – looked taller than PJ. In fact, she was about the same height as . . .

Kate flattened herself against the wall, trying to make herself invisible, holding her breath. It was Sarah! Long striped hair, rock-chick trousers. It was Sarah, no question. Kate was speechless.

Sarah and Conrad were snogging each other! Sarah didn't even like Conrad. She was always going on about what an idiot he was. It looked as if she'd had a sudden change of mind.

All the time that Kate had been going crazy with guilt, desperately trying to track her down, to confess her boyfriend-stealing crime, Sarah had been snogging Conrad. The two-timing minx . . .

Kate was too busy staring at them to notice who had followed her through the exit. Mark sneaked up behind her, grabbed her round the waist and attacked her neck with a growl.

'Come here, gorgeous, and kiss me, before somebody sees us . . .'

Kate fought him off and held him at arm's length. 'Too late!' she groaned, as Sarah and Conrad stepped out of the shadows, blinking in the light. 'I think we've just been seen.'

♥

Big Bust Up

'Mark?' Sarah stood in the light, looking dazed, letting go of Conrad's hand. 'What did you just call her? Gorgeous?'

'Uh-oh!' Mark bit his lip. 'We're really in trouble now.'

'I don't believe it.' Sarah glared angrily at Mark, then Kate, her so-called friend. 'You cow! How could you?' she fumed. 'You're supposed to be my best mate, not a boyfriend snatcher.'

'Well, excuse me,' gasped Kate. 'But I didn't notice you looking too guilty about PJ just now, when you were sticking your tongue down her boyfriend's throat.'

Sarah stood with her hands on her hips, stunned. 'That was different. It just happened. We didn't plan it.'

'Yeah, right. Tell that to PJ,' scowled Kate, grabbing Mark's hand. 'It takes a boyfriend snatcher to know a boyfriend snatcher. So that makes us even.'

'I should have known you'd do this,' Sarah

yelled. 'You flirt like a maniac with every guy you meet. Flicking your stupid hair and going all girlie.'

'So how did you end up with Conrad?' Kate shouted. 'By osmosis?'

Sarah tutted loudly. 'I only discuss my personal life with my *real* friends. Which counts you out.'

'Yeah? Well, you won't be winning any Best Friend of the Year awards either. You're as guilty as me and you know it,' Kate hissed. 'And at least I'm not trying to deny it.'

'What do you want me to do? Give you a round of applause? Great friend you turned out to be.' Sarah stepped towards Kate angrily. 'I thought I could trust you.'

'And PJ thinks she can trust you.'

Conrad stepped quickly between them before things could turn nastier. 'I thought you two were supposed to be best mates?'

'So did I,' snapped Sarah.

'Well, stop shouting at each other then and talk,' he sighed.

Kate folded her arms, saying sulkily, 'What's there to talk about?'

'Plenty,' frowned Sarah. 'Like how long have you two been seeing each other behind my back?'

'Well, how long have you been snogging Conrad?'

'Not long enough,' he murmured under his breath. And it would have been a lot longer if Kate hadn't discovered them.

Sarah turned on Mark frostily. 'At least this explains why you had to go to all those extra "rehearsals". Were you planning to tell me about Kate?' she seethed. 'Or were you just going to announce it at the end of the gig?'

Kate tutted. 'Why do you think I've been looking for you all evening, you silly cow? Why do you think I left you a note marked urgent? I waited in all day for you to ring me back.'

'Well, I did ring, this evening, but you'd already gone out.' Sarah looked at her suspiciously. 'Why was it so urgent to tell me tonight? This must have been going on for a while, right?'

'Tell her.' Mark squeezed Kate's hand. 'She'll find out anyway.'

'Find out what?'

Kate flicked her hair out of her eyes in a strop. 'Mish saw us together last night, in Mark's car. She was threatening to tell you,' she sighed. 'I didn't want you to hear it from that bitch.'

Sarah glared at her, speechless.

'Don't give me that pathetic hurt look,' Kate exploded. 'You're not exactly a perfect little angel either. I caught you snogging Conrad, remember?' Kate scowled at Conrad, who scratched his head anxiously, looking over at Mark. He had to say something. He couldn't just pinch a mate's girlfriend without even apologising.

'Sorry about this. I mean, I got the feeling you and Sarah were not really . . .'

'Romeo and Juliet?' Mark put an arm around Kate. 'Don't worry. We weren't.'

Conrad smiled, relieved. 'Great gig by the way. Did you write the new stuff?'

'I don't believe you two,' Sarah snapped suddenly. 'Who cares about the stupid gig? What about the boyfriend snatching?'

Conrad shrugged. 'What about it? Nobody really got hurt.'

'You hated coming to band meetings anyway,' Mark grinned at her cheekily. 'And Kate stopped seeing Joe ages ago.'

Sarah stared at Kate, shocked. 'You and Joe broke up?'

Kate nodded.

'See?' Mark smiled, satisfied. 'Things have worked out great for everyone.'

'Not everyone,' frowned Sarah.

'So take Mark back, if you want him so much.' Kate took his hand and held it out to her.

Sarah stepped back and studied him critically. Scruffy jeans, messy hair, trainers about to fall apart at the seams. What had she ever seen in him in the first place? He was totally the wrong image for her. How could she get serious about a guy who wrote 'SEXY' across his chest with a black marker pen?

'You're welcome to him,' she said, pushing his hand away. 'He was a lousy boyfriend anyway.'

Mark looked hurt. 'I wasn't that bad.'

'So why did you try to cripple me on our first date?' Sarah asked.

Mark ran a hand through his hair. 'All I did was take you ice-skating.'

'Exactly. It took my ankles weeks to recover.'

'Look, maybe the guys have got a point,' Kate interrupted loudly, before another row started up. 'This is stupid. I mean, what are we even arguing about? Everyone has got what they wanted, haven't they?'

Sarah opened her mouth to speak, then shut it again. She hated to admit it, but Kate was right. So what if Kate was seeing Mark? Sarah had been planning to dump him anyway. He'd been a lot of fun, at first. But she'd soon realised Mark lived on planet shallow. The Judes might be cool, but Mark was unreliable, and prone to long, boring speeches about his car. How could anyone care so much about a stupid heap of metal? He talked to his convertible more than to her.

She'd had no idea about Kate and Mark, though. How could she have missed it? She should have guessed. Mark was always out. Kate kept dashing off after college. It all made perfect sense now.

And Kate was doing her a huge favour. She could stop pretending to be interested in spark plugs and concentrate on Conrad. The real guy of her dreams. She gripped Kate's arm and took her to one side. She hated fighting with Kate anyway. Kate always won. 'I'm not sorry I yelled at you,' she said moodily. 'I meant every word. You deserved it.'

'So did you.' Kate prodded her shoulder. 'Call me a cow again and I'll break all your nails off.'

Sarah quickly hid her hands in her pockets. She'd been growing her nails for ages. 'I guess this is pretty stupid.' She smiled up at Kate reluctantly. 'Are we still friends?'

'Only if you get on our knees and beg for forgiveness.'

'Get lost!' Sarah tugged her hair playfully. 'You should be apologising to me. And if I ever catch you flirting with Conrad . . .'

Kate studied him over her shoulder. 'Don't worry,' she grinned. 'I prefer guys who work up a sweat chasing *me* around, not a football.' She hugged Sarah warmly, relieved. Things could have been a real mess, with badly damaged feelings on both sides. But somehow, she'd managed to keep her best mate and Mark. Kate was one lucky girl.

'Want to hear what happened before you came outside and put your big foot in it?' Sarah laughed.

Kate's face lit up. They hadn't had a proper

gossip about lads for weeks. They had a lot of catching up to do. But first, they had to get rid of the guys.

She skipped back over to Mark and stroked his shoulder. 'Could you and Conrad go for a beer or something? Sarah and I have to talk.'

Mark looked surprised. 'I thought you just did?'

'Don't lads understand anything?' Sarah tutted behind him. 'It's going to take us at least an hour to pull you to pieces.'

Mark looked alarmed. 'Why, what have I done?'

'She's just kidding,' Kate whispered in his ear. 'She's going to dish the dirt on Conrad. We're saving you for tomorrow.'

She kissed his cheek, giggling, linked arms with Sarah and disappeared back inside.

'Girls!' Conrad appeared beside Mark grinning. 'Nothing but trouble, man.'

Mark nodded, puzzled. 'Why do they have to make everything so complicated?'

'They're just born that way, I guess,' Conrad joked. 'I wonder what they're saying about us?'

'It's probably better if we don't know.' Mark took off his jacket and tied it round his waist. 'Shall we go for a drink?' He didn't know much about Conrad, except that he was the king of beach volleyball, but if he could cope with Sarah, he deserved an award. Mark had never been able to make out what she was going on about.

'So when Sarah gets all spiritual,' he said, as they headed towards the bar. 'Do you actually understand her . . . ?'

Kate and Sarah found a table in a deserted corner up in the gallery, where they could talk in private, without half the college listening in. They'd never believe it anyway. Kate was still in shock herself. Sarah and Conrad! They were the most unlikely couple ever.

'So come on, tell me everything,' Kate grinned excitedly, before they'd even sat down. 'I thought you hated the guy. You called him obnoxious at that footy match.'

'That was before I really got to know him,' Sarah smiled.

Kate shuffled closer, resting her elbows on the table. She had to hear this. Conrad wasn't the kind of guy Sarah usually dated. What did she see in him? Apart from a full six feet of toned muscles, of course.

'How well do you know him now?' she giggled. 'I want details.'

'Stop asking me questions and I might tell you,' grinned Sarah. 'He's been flirting with me for ages. Just harmless stuff. I ignored him mostly. But that made him worse. As if he couldn't believe any girl could possibly resist him.'

'Why didn't you tell me he was flirting?' Kate gasped.

'There was nothing much to tell. He was just being a pain. Then last Monday, the day you, me and PJ had lunch on the sports field,' Sarah paused to check no one was listening, 'he waited for me outside the Art block after lessons.'

'Oh my God!' shrieked Kate. 'And he snogged you among the paint pots?'

'No.' Sarah tapped her leg. 'He just wanted to talk about PJ.'

'And you fell for that one?' snorted Kate.

'Well, it made sense,' Sarah tutted. 'Me and PJ had already seen him once that day, right after we left you on the field.' She wrinkled up her nose, remembering how sweaty he'd been.

'They'd sort of had an argument. He wanted my advice. So he took me to that new French pâtisserie in town, for a coffee.'

Kate raised her eyebrows. 'Ooh là là! *Très* romantic.'

'All we did was talk.' Sarah sighed, going into a dreamy trance. Kate nudged her out of it. 'About what?'

'I told you, PJ. He thought I might understand her.'

'Is he crazy?' Kate giggled. 'Nobody understands PJ.'

'That's what I tried to tell him, but he still wanted my advice.'

'Are you sure that's all he wanted?' Kate asked.

Sarah had thought the same at first, that it was just another excuse for flirting. Not that Conrad needed an excuse. Flirting came more naturally to him than breathing or picking his nose.

That's why she'd snapped at him as they'd walked into the pâtisserie. 'You know this is getting really boring? I'm not impressed, OK? So you can stop acting about.'

'I was just being friendly,' he'd shrugged, checking his hair in the window.

He was unbelievable. Talk about vain. Even Sarah didn't spend that much time looking in a mirror.

She'd looked at her watch and sighed, 'If you want to talk about PJ, can you get on with it? I have things to do.'

'So leave,' he'd said moodily.

Impossible. She was far too curious. PJ never told her anything about Conrad. If there was even a minuscule chance that he was about to spill the beans, she had to stay.

She'd decided to give him ten minutes maximum, to come up with something juicy.

'Sorry,' he'd apologised quickly. 'It's just that

I've made a total mess of things with PJ.' He'd given her a sheepish smile. 'I guess I took her for granted . . .'

As soon as he'd started talking, something incredibly strange had happened. His voice, suddenly so soft and quiet, had given her actual goose-bumps, all over. She'd tried to shake it off, but his gentle, melted chocolate tones had trickled smoothly down her throat, and straight into her blood stream. Like an instant love connection.

By the third cup of coffee, she'd been drooling over his cute smile and gorgeous eyes, as if she was seeing them for the first time.

'I should have made more of an effort with PJ,' he'd sighed. 'But she didn't give me a chance. She just made up her mind that the only thing I cared about was sport.'

'Well, is it?' Sarah had asked, but she'd known the answer already. Conrad was a huge emotional gâteau, just waiting to be defrosted and devoured. There was so much more to him than a sporty body and a talent for flirting. He had a hidden side that was deeper than an olympic diving pool.

She'd fallen for him right there, in the pâtisserie. She couldn't help it. He was so sweet and sensitive. How come she'd never seen it before?

He'd looked at her, smiling. 'Are you planning to drink that coffee? Or are you just going to sit there and stir it all night?'

Sarah had put down the spoon, embarrassed. 'So what are you going to do?'

'About PJ?' he'd sighed, looking confused. 'I don't know. One minute she's all aloof and moody, the next she's cute and cuddly. What am I supposed to think?'

Sarah couldn't help. Conrad was the guy she'd been looking for. He took her seriously. He wanted to talk about the deeper side of life. And Mark . . . ?

Sarah grinned at Kate across the table and yelled above the noise of the club, 'No offence, but Mark thinks having a deep and meaningful conversation involves talking about spare parts for his car.'

'That's what I like in a guy,' Kate giggled. 'Less talking, more time for snogging.'

'You would!' Sarah rolled her eyes. 'I need a guy who can give me something back. You wouldn't believe how sensitive he is.'

'Who, Conrad?' Kate almost choked. 'Are you sure? He doesn't look that sensitive on a footie field.'

'Well, he wouldn't, would he?' Sarah picked at a beer mat absently. 'He's different when you get him alone.'

'Wait!' Kate grabbed her arm. 'You mean he talked about actual emotions?'

Sarah nodded. 'It was like a dam bursting or something. I couldn't get a word in.' She smiled, remembering. 'He'd kill me if he knew I was telling you this.'

'I won't tell a soul,' Kate promised, crossing her heart. 'What happened after coffee? Did he walk you home and give your lips a good seeing to?'

Sarah shrugged. 'I went home alone, and finished my Art project.'

'After he'd said all that? Didn't you even hold hands or hug?' Kate looked disappointed.

'We weren't ready for that. Besides, he's still seeing PJ. I couldn't exactly leap over the table and snog his face off.'

'I bet he wouldn't have put up much of a fight,' Kate smiled. 'So when did he start getting physical?'

Sarah cupped her chin in her hands. 'It all happened so quickly. I've seen him every day this week, out of college, but we didn't do anything until today,' she grinned. 'I met him in town this morning.'

'I thought you were shopping for boots?'

'That was just a cover story,' said Sarah.

Kate was going to kill her. She'd been at home for hours, going crazy with guilt, and all the time, Sarah had been with another guy.

'Then I met him out at the back this evening after PJ had gone, and that's when you appeared.' Sarah looked embarrassed. 'Right in the middle of our first kiss.'

Kate grinned. 'You should have picked some-where more private if you didn't want an audience.' Finally they were getting down to the nitty gritty. She leaned forward eagerly. 'What was he like? Does he floss his teeth, or did you do it for him?'

'Don't be so gross,' Sarah giggled.

It had been an incredible night. Conrad had looked amazing, his white T-shirt all rippled with shadows and muscle.

'It's very dark out here. You'd better stay close,' he'd whispered, sliding his fingers down her bare arm and holding her hand tight. 'It's taken me weeks to get you alone. I don't want to lose you now.'

She'd been desperate to snog him for days. But every time they'd come close, she'd pulled away guiltily, reminding herself that Conrad was PJ's boyfriend. It was wrong even to dream about kissing him.

'Sorry.' She'd let go of his hand with a sigh. But Conrad had pulled her back again. 'Worry about PJ tomorrow,' he'd whispered, touching her face. 'Just one little kiss . . . ?'

What was a girl supposed to do? Conrad was too close, too perfect to refuse again. She had to know what it felt like.

It had been the most amazing kiss ever. Most guys were more worried about doing it right than enjoying the actual kiss. But Conrad had attacked her lips like a mad snog fiend: gentle, then passionate, then playful. They were just getting to an interesting point when Kate had caught them.

Kate stared at Sarah open-mouthed. 'He sounds incredible.'

Sarah hugged herself with a dreamy sigh. 'He held me really gently. Then we got closer and closer, and his hands were round my face, stroking my neck, and it was just so . . .'

'Stop!' Kate gasped. 'You're making me go all gooey.'

'My lips are still tingling,' Sarah touched her face the way Conrad had, with the tips of his fingers. 'He must have mini-electrodes in his lips or something. Do mine look any different?'

She leant closer so that Kate could see them properly under the light.

'What am I looking for exactly?' Kate screwed up her eyes, concentrating.

'Just tell me if they've changed.'

'They look really pink,' Kate grinned. 'But that's probably just lipstick.'

Sarah got a tiny mirror out of her pocket and studied them closely.

Kate laughed. 'I felt exactly the same way the first time I kissed Mark.'

Sarah stopped staring at her lips and looked at Kate. 'You know, you two are so well suited.

Aquarius and Scorpio, strong physical attraction, the classic recipe for long-lasting love. I really should have guessed.'

'Well, I'm glad you didn't,' Kate sighed. 'We just couldn't stop it from happening. It must have been fate or something.'

Sarah frowned. 'You don't believe in fate. You're always saying it's a load of rubbish.'

'Maybe I was wrong. Mark makes me laugh. And he's so full of surprises.'

'Don't you think he's kind of . . . immature?' Sarah asked carefully.

'All guys are immature,' Kate grinned. 'It's genetic. But at least Mark doesn't try to hide it. Anyway,' she laughed, 'I like the way he messes around.'

Sarah scowled. 'I hated that. I never knew what he was going to do next.'

'Exactly. That's what makes him so exciting.'

'I still says he's immature,' Sarah smiled. 'He couldn't even keep a straight face when we were kissing.'

Kate played coyly with her hair. 'I've never had that problem.' Just the opposite in fact. Mark was the ultimate snog experience.

'What would you have done if I'd taken him back just now?' Sarah teased.

Kate shrugged. 'I knew you wouldn't.' Besides, Mark might have had a few objections.

'And what happened to Joe?' asked Sarah, curiously. 'I thought he was your perfect guy?'

Kate cringed. 'More like the biggest mistake of my life. I almost fell asleep on our first date.' She shook her head slowly. 'I need a guy who'll leave me breathless, not snoozing into my starter.'

Sarah rolled her eyes. 'Don't be so cruel. I like Joe. He's a nice guy.'

'Nice but dull.'

'So why did you let us go on thinking he was still your boyfriend?'

'I thought if I told you, you'd accuse me of being shallow,' Kate admitted. 'You and PJ are always teasing me about my short-term boyfriends.'

Sarah gave her hand a squeeze. 'That's one of the things we love about you, silly. Your amazing ability to get over lads in like, two hours.'

'I guess I'm just lucky that way,' Kate giggled, 'but it's different with Mark.'

Sarah buried her face in her hands and groaned.

'It's true,' Kate hit her arm. 'Mark and I are really close.'

Sarah pulled her over, whispering urgently, 'I believe you. But we haven't got time to discuss it now. Look who's coming this way.'

Kate turned round in her seat. It was Mish. She'd finally tracked them down. She dedicated her whole life to spoiling other people's fun.

'God, doesn't she ever give up?' Kate sighed. 'She's been bugging me all night. We'll never get rid of her now.'

Mish stood between them, with a malicious smile. Her face was hot and sweaty from searching.

'What are you two doing all huddled up together in a corner? Flipping a coin to see who gets Mark?' She folded her arms smugly. 'I presume you have told Sarah I caught you hijacking her boyfriend in his car last night?'

'What do you think?' Kate studied her fingernails casually. 'Anyway, you're wasting your time. Sarah and I have agreed to share Mark.'

She kicked Sarah under the table. Mish could be so gullible. If she was looking for gossip, they'd give her the twenty-four carat variety. 'Sarah's still his official girlfriend. I'm on standby for weekends and special occasions.'

'You can see him on Wednesday evenings too, if you like. For band rehearsals,' Sarah winked back. 'I've got better things to do than listen to that lot arguing about whose turn it is to go out for burgers.'

'Well, only if you're sure,' Kate said in a serious voice.

Mish stared wide-eyed at Kate, then Sarah. 'You're winding me up, right? You two would never share a guy.'

'Why not?' Kate shrugged.

'Because it's illegal or something,' Mish spluttered, pulling up a chair and sitting down. 'Don't you think that Mark might notice he's got more than one girlfriend?'

'It was his idea,' Sarah whispered.

'Yeah,' Kate added. 'He couldn't choose between us, so he had this great idea for a timeshare. I don't know why we didn't think of it sooner.'

Mish stared at them, shocked. 'You can't snog the same guy, it's unhygienic.'

'Don't worry, we've got it all worked out. He gets a day off every Thursday,' Sarah said. 'Just don't tell anybody, OK?'

Kate bit on a beer mat, smothering a fit of the giggles. Sarah stared up at the ceiling, trying hard not to crack up.

Mish suddenly shot up. 'You two are sick,' she hissed, looking flustered, stumbling over a chair. 'Somebody should report you . . .'

Kate burst out laughing as she disappeared down the stairs. 'Did you see her face?' she shrieked. 'She was practically having a baby. I thought she was going to pass out.'

Sarah flicked a stray crisp at her across the table. 'If you hadn't started sniggering, she would have believed us.'

'Thank God she doesn't know about Conrad.' Kate wiped the tears out of her eyes. 'She'd have been on the phone to PJ right now.'

Sarah handed her a tissue. 'Thanks for reminding me.'

PJ still liked Conrad. 'He's so sweet.' That's what she'd said earlier that evening, when Sarah had tried to get something out of her. 'So sweet' meant PJ still had feelings for him. It also meant Sarah had done an unforgivable thing.

'What am I going to do?' she moaned guiltily.

Kate sighed. 'Has PJ said anything else to you about Conrad?'

Sarah shook her head. 'You know PJ, she's keeping everything to herself, as usual. Even Conrad's not sure how she feels about him.'

'You could move to another country,' Kate joked. 'I hear South America's nice at this time of year.'

Sarah glared at her. 'I'm being serious, Kate.'

'Sorry, I was just trying to make you laugh.' Now that the heat was off, she was back to her old self.

'It isn't funny, OK?' Sarah shifted round in her chair and leant back against the wall. 'People expect you to steal boyfriends and stuff. But PJ trusts me.'

'Thanks a lot,' Kate said, hurt. 'You make it sound like I do this all the time.'

Sarah sighed heavily. 'You have to help me. I don't know what to do.'

'There's only one thing you can do,' Kate said. 'Tell her.'

'You didn't tell me,' Sarah snapped.

'True. But look at the mess it got me into with Mish? Do you want her to find out about this little scandal too?'

Sarah fidgeted restlessly, tapping the table top with her fingers. 'I don't have much choice do I?'

'You and PJ are really close. You owe her the truth.'

'And you owe me a favour. You can't just pinch my boyfriend and expect to get away with it,' frowned Sarah.

'Can't I?' sighed Kate. 'So what exactly do you want me to do?'

'Be there when I tell her. I need all the help I can get.'

Kate nodded. It was the least she could do. After all, Sarah had been pretty understanding about Mark – eventually. She was a real friend. And that was worth a bit of support, even on a Sunday.

'The boys are coming back over,' Sarah nodded towards the gallery stairs. Mark and Conrad were approaching cautiously.

'Is everything OK?' asked Mark. 'I just saw Mish. She called me a loser and thumped me.' He rubbed his bruised arm.

'Don't be such a baby,' Kate teased. 'If it hurts that much get Conrad to kiss it better.'

Mark rolled his sleeve down again quickly.

'What have you two been talking about?' asked Sarah.

Conrad yawned. 'You know, just footie, cars and some other stuff.'

'Like which one of you two is the best kisser,' Mark grinned.

Sarah squeezed Conrad's knee under the table. 'That all depends on the person who's kissing you back.'

'I'm starving,' Mark said. 'Does anyone want to go and get some food?'

'Sure.' Conrad stood up and grabbed Sarah's hand.

'Don't,' she whispered, untangling their fingers quickly. 'Somebody might see us.'

Conrad let her go and followed her down the stairs. Sarah had driven him wild for weeks, acting all indifferent and uninterested. He didn't want to ruin it all now.

She was the most gorgeous girl he'd ever kissed. She looked great too. But she wasn't just into clothes. She had loads of interesting stuff to talk about: dreams, astrology, books, life, art. He could totally be himself when she was around. Say things he usually kept inside.

He could never be so open with PJ. He had a feeling she didn't want him to get that close. She was still a total mystery. How many people got to see the real PJ, Conrad wondered? Not many. Kate and Sarah, maybe.

Still, he didn't exactly feel great about cheating on her. 'What are we going to do about PJ?' he said quietly. 'We have to tell her.'

Sarah nodded. 'Let me do it.'

She wanted PJ to understand her feelings for Conrad. That it wasn't just a casual fling. She might have to say some embarrassing stuff. She could only go through with it if Conrad wasn't there.

'Are you sorry you kissed me?' he whispered, resting his hands on Sarah's hips.

'No,' she smiled. It had been the most amazing kiss ever. She'd be in heaven if it wasn't for the after-shock of guilt. She tapped Kate on the shoulder as they pushed through the gig room, towards the main entrance. 'Can I come round early tomorrow? So we can figure out what to do about PJ?'

Kate nodded. She wasn't looking forward to it. She'd already been through one boyfriend trauma, but two in twenty-four hours? It was too much for any girl.

'I've got to go round the back to pick up my stuff.' Mark squeezed Kate's hand. 'Come with me. I'll introduce you to the guys this time. They're friendlier than they look.'

Kate grinned. Now that she was Mark's only, official girlfriend, she might as well flaunt it. Let everyone know she was dating the bassist. That they were crazy about each other.

She grabbed hold of his ear and pulled him closer for a kiss. 'What was that for?' he grinned, wiping lipstick off his mouth with the back of his hand.

'I was just thinking how lucky you are to be with me,' she teased. 'Did Sarah get on with the Judes?'

Mark thought for a second. 'She never really tried. She sat in a corner looking fed up most of the time.'

'Poor Sarah,' Kate sighed. She'd been expecting a major image boost, a one-way ticket to glamour. Instead, she'd got landed with a bunch of scruffy gits.

Kate couldn't wait to meet them. For a bunch of scruffy gits, they looked like they knew how to have fun.

Sarah and Conrad were waiting for them outside by Mark's car. 'We've changed our minds about the food,' Conrad said sleepily. 'I'm going to walk Sarah home instead.'

Sarah's head was throbbing. Everything was happening too quickly. The kiss, the row, the after-effects. She couldn't cope with food right now. She needed to be alone with Conrad. To make sure he was serious about her. Before she dropped her little bombshell on poor PJ.

Sarah felt sick. Tomorrow was going to arrive way too quickly for comfort.

♥

All's Fair

'Wait!' Sarah grabbed the phone out of Kate's hand and held it way above her head, out of reach. 'I've changed my mind. I'll tell her tomorrow. I'm not ready yet.'

'Tell her tomorrow?' Kate gasped. 'In college, with the whole coffee bar watching? Get real, Sarah. You might as well make a documentary and put it out on TV.'

Sarah sighed. 'I didn't think about it like that.'

'Well it's a good job one of us did.' Kate put an arm around her shoulders. 'The longer you leave it, the worse it gets. I should know. I've been through the whole drama, remember? Just let me ring her.'

Sarah put the phone down reluctantly. 'OK. But I have to speak to Conrad first.'

'Again?' She'd already phoned him once that morning, as soon as she'd arrived at Kate's house. When Sarah had a crisis, she milked it like a herd of dairy cows.

'Can't you save all that slushy stuff for later?' she asked.

Sarah glared at her. 'No. And it's not slush, OK?'

'Fine.' Kate gave up and stomped into the kitchen. 'Just make it quick. Before I totally lose my patience.'

'What patience?' Sarah yelled after her, dialling Conrad's number. 'You never had any in the first place.'

So what if she'd already phoned him? Was there a law against talking to her new man? Only in Kate's house. And just because Sarah didn't handle things Kate's way, she was getting stroppy.

Tough. Kate had promised to help her and she'd better start helping soon.

'Hello?' Conrad sounded rushed and flustered.

'What's wrong?' she asked.

'Last minute basketball practice. I have to go in, like, three minutes. Will you be OK? Have you phoned her yet?'

'Almost,' Sarah sighed. 'Kate dialled four digits this time before I made her stop.'

'I feel really bad about leaving you to do this alone. Can I come round tonight and see you?' he asked eagerly.

His gorgeous voice made Sarah tingle. He could come round any time, day or night. 'I should be home by six o'clock. Come round when you like.'

'OK, I'll ring you. And Sarah,' he hesitated, 'don't worry. Everything will be all right.'

That was easy for him to say. He wasn't about to face PJ with the awful truth. 'Worry about PJ tomorrow,' he'd said last night, before they'd kissed. Well, she was worried. PJ didn't show strong emotions but they were definitely there, bubbling under the surface. She'd probably go away and brood over it for weeks, then suddenly ignore her in college one day and that would be it. Friendship – *au revoir*. No second chances.

'I'll be thinking about you,' said Conrad softly.

Sarah couldn't help smiling. 'Any bit of me in particular?'

'Ask me later and I'll show you,' he teased. 'See you this evening.'

She put the phone down. Kate appeared from the kitchen and handed her a coffee. 'Peace offering,' she grinned sheepishly. 'Sorry I've been a bit snappy.'

'A bit?' Sarah snorted.

'OK, I've been a total pain in the butt,' Kate admitted. 'But I got to bed really late. And my ears are still buzzing from the gig last night.'

'Just stop taking it out on me,' Sarah pushed her. 'I've got enough to cope with already.'

Kate grinned at her. 'So what now?' They hovered uneasily by the phone. Kate picked up the receiver. 'Shall I ring PJ, or not? It's up to you.'

Sarah nodded slowly. 'Do it before I change my mind again.'

She sat on the stairs, gripping her coffee tightly and letting Kate ring the whole number this time.

'Oh my God, it's ringing,' Kate hissed. 'What do I say if she answers . . . PJ?'

Sarah felt sick. That morning she'd rung a horoscope line for an emergency reading. Things didn't look good. Taurians were advised to 'stay in bed to avoid disasters with long-lasting side-effects'.

PJ's horoscope was even worse. 'You lose your temper today, and under the circumstances, nobody will blame you. Even mild Librans have their limits, and today, you get pushed way beyond yours by a not-so-perfect friend.' It was a sign. A sign that PJ was going to kill her.

How could everything be so wonderful and dreamy with Conrad. And such a mess with PJ?

'She's turning down the volume on her tape deck,' said Kate, covering the mouthpiece with her hand. 'Shall I tell her you're here?'

Sarah shook her head. PJ wasn't stupid. She'd be able to tell something was wrong from Sarah's shaky voice. She couldn't tell PJ over the phone. If she was going to do it at all, it had to be in person.

'I'm fine,' Kate said suddenly. PJ was back on the other end of the line. 'Yeah, last night was great,' she went on, pulling a face at Sarah. 'That's sort of why I'm ringing. Do you want to come and meet Sarah and me? We can tell you all the gossip then.' Sarah held her breath.

'No, I can't really tell you over the phone. It's kind of . . . delicate.' Kate was trying to choose her words carefully. 'Let's go for some food. We used to do that all the time on a Sunday.' She paused, listening. 'The new French pâtisserie in town?'

Sarah stood up in a panic, waving her arms urgently at Kate. 'No, not there!' she hissed. Anywhere but the pâtisserie. That was the last place on earth she wanted to meet PJ. She'd been there with Conrad, drooling over his sexy voice. It wouldn't be right. She felt guilty enough already.

'Two o'clock's fine,' Kate said, ignoring her. 'We'll meet you inside.'

She put down the phone, cringing. 'That was awful. I felt like a criminal. She definitely knows something's wrong. She kept asking me why I sounded funny.'

Sarah banged her coffee mug down on the hall table. 'Never mind that. You know I can't meet her in the pâtisserie.'

'OK, don't get hysterical,' sighed Kate. 'It was PJ's idea. What was I supposed to say? Sorry, PJ, but that's a no-go area because Sarah chatted up your boyfriend in there just last week?' She took Sarah into the lounge and sat her down. 'Forget the venue. Do you know what you're going to say to her?'

'How would *you* tell her?' asked Sarah, anxiously.

Kate thought for a second, playing with her pendant. 'I'd probably sit snogging a photo of Conrad, right in front of her, and hope she got the message.'

'Miss Subtlety strikes again,' Sarah smiled.

Kate perched on the arm of the chair beside her. 'Practise what you're going to say on me. I'll pretend to be PJ.'

'Kate, you're nothing like her,' Sarah giggled. 'PJ's quiet and reserved.' And Kate definitely wasn't.

'Well, have you got any better ideas?' She jumped up and disappeared into the hall, shutting the door.

'What are you doing now?' Sarah called after her, puzzled.

Kate burst back into the lounge. 'I'm being PJ. Pretend this is the café and I'm her, just walking in.'

She sat on the sofa facing Sarah, fiddling with her hair, the way PJ always did when she was concentrating.

'This is stupid, I can't do it,' Sarah tutted.

'OK, I'll start you off. You've got something to tell me?'

'Are you being PJ now?' asked Sarah, confused.

Kate nodded. 'We haven't got much time, so just get on with it.'

♥ 133 ♥

Sarah sipped her coffee. Anything was worth a try. 'OK,' she said, clearing her throat. 'PJ, it's about Conrad.'

'You bitch! I thought I could trust you!' Kate stormed out of the lounge. 'I never want to speak to you again.' She slammed the door, then peeped back into the room. 'How was I?'

Sarah glared at her. 'I haven't even said it yet. This isn't a game, Kate. If you're going to act like an idiot, just forget it.'

'Sorry. I got a bit carried away. PJ wouldn't do that, would she?' Kate sat down again and crossed her legs. 'OK, let's try again.'

Sarah sighed impatiently. 'Conrad and me . . . no that's not right. PJ,' she said seriously, 'this is really hard to say, but . . . That's not right either.'

'Just spit it out,' Kate laughed, chucking a cushion at her. 'She'll have given up and gone home before you've said anything at this rate.'

'I know, can I have another go?' Sarah groaned. It was harder than she'd thought to put it into words. She couldn't just say, 'Conrad fancies me now, so sorry, but he's dumping you.' She didn't want to hurt PJ any more than she had to. 'I'm just going to say it straight out.' She put her hands flat on her knees. 'PJ, you're not going to believe this, but I kissed Conrad last night.'

'Go on,' Kate encouraged her. 'You've really got it this time.'

'It wasn't an accident,' she went on. 'I knew exactly what I was doing and how much it would hurt you. You can hate me, if you want. I probably deserve it. But it's like, me and Conrad were meant to be together.' Sarah stopped and held her head in her hands. 'I can't say that, it's awful.'

'No, it was brilliant!' Kate gasped. 'Now it's my turn. You and Conrad, the kiss, blah blah blah . . .' She had to try to react like PJ. It wasn't easy. 'OK,' she said, 'this is me being PJ again . . . Why isn't Conrad here?'

Sarah shrugged. 'I wanted to tell you alone. We've been friends for so long.'

'It's a pity you didn't think about that when you were snogging my boyfriend.'

'I did think about it,' Sarah said.

'And it still didn't stop you?' Kate flicked her hair. 'Our friendship obviously doesn't mean that much to you.'

Sarah looked upset. 'Of course it does. Do you really think PJ will say that?'

Kate stood up. 'How should I know?'

'What if she doesn't even give me a chance to explain. What if she just cries? Or tells everyone in college what a cow I am?' Sarah gripped the cushion beside her in a sudden panic. 'I've just had a horrible thought.'

'What?'

'Do you remember last term, when Pauline from college found out that Howard was two-timing her, with Emma *and* Heather?'

Kate grinned. 'How could I forget? She hung all those grotty grey underpants in the tree outside the Art room, and told everyone they were his?' she giggled. 'He couldn't get another girlfriend for months. Served him right.'

Sarah looked pale. 'Well, what if PJ wants revenge? She's got photos of me, when I was still at school, wearing seriously embarrassing trousers.'

'So?' Kate shrugged.

'Don't you see?' Sarah panicked. 'She could pin them up in the coffee bar. Or get them made up into T-shirts and give them to the footie team?'

Kate grabbed the cushion out of her grasp before she squeezed it to death. 'Sarah, stop over-reacting. PJ wouldn't be so mean. Mind you . . .'

'What?' Sarah snapped.

'Sharon's a bit like PJ, and she didn't take it too well when she caught Jonathan snogging her mate Fiona, at the college Christmas do.'

'Oh God, I remember.' Sarah went even paler. 'She went completely berserk by the buffet and poured that trifle down Jonathan's jeans. In front of everyone.'

Kate nodded seriously. 'It's always the quiet ones.'

'PJ wouldn't do that – would she?'

'What do we know about the real PJ? I mean, what actually goes on in her mind?' Kate frowned.

'Search me? I'm only her best friend. How should I know?'

Sarah grabbed another cushion and hugged it tightly. She felt ten times worse now, thanks to Kate and her stupid idea of role playing. She should have gone hysterical and had a good panic instead. Or told Conrad it was over. Anything was easier to bear than this awful guilt.

Kate checked her watch. 'I'd better go and get my jacket.'

She left Sarah in the lounge and dashed up the stairs, feeling totally drained. Why did Sarah have to get so intense about everything? She was too deep for her own good. Kate preferred to let problems solve themselves. But she couldn't abandon Sarah now. A promise was a promise. And Sarah needed her.

The tiny chocolate heart Mark had given her was on the bedside table. She brushed it with her fingers as she walked past. Last night, after the gig and the whole Sarah/Conrad commotion, she'd gone backstage with him to pick up his stuff.

She'd met the rest of the Judes properly. They were a mad bunch of guys. Telling her hilarious stories about Mark's band auditions, and how he could only play one song, 'Happy Birthday'.

'That's a total lie,' he'd grinned, embarrassed. 'They're just jealous 'cos I get all the girls.'

'Get any girls while I'm around and you're dead,' she'd joked, poking him in the ribs.

He'd dragged her into a quiet corner, whispering, 'Do you want to hear something new I wrote?'

'Shall I call the rest of the guys over?' she'd asked.

'He'd shaken his head. 'It's not for the Judes.'

He'd played her the bass line of a sweet love song, about a girl. He looked so gorgeous, picking out the notes, messy hair falling across his face, all mean and moody in the shadows. She'd wanted to stop him mid-chorus for a snog.

'Can you play "Old MacDonald had a Farm" too?' she'd giggled, when he'd finished.

'You didn't like it?' He'd scratched his head, looking disappointed. 'I kind of wrote it for you.'

'I'm the girl in the song?' She'd almost passed out on the spot. Mark never told her how he felt. But he could write it all down in a ballad and sing it? It didn't make sense. Still, she wasn't complaining.

'I loved it, idiot.' She'd squashed him against the wall with a passionate kiss. 'Play it again.'

He'd promised to play it for her in private tonight. She couldn't wait. Her own little love song. It was far better than a tacky pair of earrings or a CD. Just wait until she told Sarah. She'd be so jealous.

Mark was one boyfriend Kate was planning to hang onto for a long time. Tonight, it was her turn to surprise him. She'd found the perfect present to thank him for the song. Chocolate flavoured lip paint. Brush it on. Snog it off.

She grabbed her jacket and raced down the stairs again. Sarah was hugging her knees.

'Are you ready?' Kate handed Sarah her bag.

'I'll never be ready,' Sarah frowned, clutching her stomach. 'Let's just get this over with before I throw up.'

She still felt nauseous on the bus. It was like going to the dentist, only without the anaesthetic. Kate was cracking stupid jokes, trying to keep her cheerful. It wasn't working.

'If you were a real friend, you'd tell her for me,' said Sarah, hopefully.

'No way!' Kate squeezed her hand. 'I'm not a "break it gently" kind of girl.'

'True,' Sarah sighed. Kate was unpredictable in a crisis. Just like a tropical storm, full of wind and fury. She'd probably say something stupid and make things worse.

*

They got to the pâtisserie ten minutes early. Kate found a window table so that they could see PJ coming, and ordered two coffees.

'So is this the table where you and Conrad sat?' she hissed.

'It's over there.' Sarah gazed at their special corner, where she'd first realised how perfect Conrad was. Most guys dropped dead with fright if she ever mentioned things like 'feelings'. They were terrified of confessing they had any. But with Conrad, it was different. Like peeling an onion and finding a tasty truffle inside.

The pâtisserie should put a gold placard on the wall above the very spot where it all happened, saying, 'Table of love'. Or maybe after today, the inscription should read, 'Dedicated to Sarah. Tragically murdered by PJ for stealing her boyfriend.'

'They'd never get all that on a placard,' Kate grinned.

Sarah wished Conrad was with her now. Why had she decided to tell PJ on her own? She must have been mad. They should have phoned her last night, together. Then emigrated.

'Do you want another practice?' asked Kate, scanning the room for familiar faces. Sophie and Denise from college were just paying by the till . . . 'Oh no,' she whispered. 'I don't believe it. Joe's here too.'

He was almost hidden behind a plant, tucking into a huge club sandwich. Hopefully, he hadn't noticed them coming in. That was all Kate needed to round off her day, another exciting encounter with Mr Personality.

'Who cares about Joe? I want to go home,' Sarah moaned. 'We could leave now, before she arrives.'

Kate pinned her arm to the table. 'Just stay calm and try not to look so guilty.'

'So what do you want me to do? Get up on the table and dance?' Sarah hissed.

'There's no time for that,' Kate lowered her voice. 'PJ's just walked past the window.'

Sarah panicked. 'Don't let her come in. Tell her I'm sick, anything. Just give me time to get away.' She grabbed Kate's sleeve. 'I could write her a letter instead, in fact, that's a much better idea anyway. I can handle this on paper.'

It was too late. PJ was already inside, looking far too cheerful and heading straight for their table.

'Hey, you two!' She sat down next to Sarah. 'Have you seen the dishy waiter?' She craned her neck round to look at him serving coffee at the next table. 'Is he gorgeous or what?'

'Stunning,' Kate mumbled.

'I like this place already,' PJ grinned, peeling off her jacket. 'Have you two ordered? Are we going for cakes and coffee?'

'Just coffee,' Sarah sighed. She still felt sick. The sight of a cream cake might push her over the edge. She was determined not to throw up in the pâtisserie. She'd never live it down.

'We haven't done this for ages.' PJ studied the menu. 'I'm glad you phoned. It's really cosy in here.'

She looked up. Sarah was gazing out of the window in a trance. Kate had been stirring her coffee for five minutes. PJ suddenly got the feeling that she'd been talking to herself since she walked in.

'OK, what's up with you two?' She folded up the menu. 'I thought you were desperate to tell me what happened at the gig last night?'

Sarah went white and stared down at the sugar bowl. If Kate created a diversion now, she could slide out under the table and escape through the kitchens. It could be done. She was sure of it.

'So come on then.' PJ was getting impatient. 'Are you going to dish the dirt or not?'

Kate shrugged. 'What do you want to know? The Judes were absolutely brilliant.'

'That's not gossip,' PJ said. 'I want names, times, places. Who did I miss doing what?'

'Well,' Kate attempted to approach the subject carefully. 'Joe was there, and Mish.'

'Oh, God,' PJ interrupted her. 'I've just remembered. I was about to leave last night, and Mish dragged me back inside and said something strange about Mark.'

'You should tell PJ about Mark,' Sarah said quickly to Kate.

Kate frowned. 'Isn't there something you'd like to say first?'

Sarah shook her head. 'It can wait.' It could wait forever as far as Sarah was concerned. The longer the better.

'Me and Mark,' Kate paused. 'Well, we've kind of been seeing each other for weeks.'

PJ glanced quickly at Sarah. 'But I thought you and Mark . . .'

'So did I. Until last night.'

'Sarah found out by accident,' explained Kate. 'But she's been great about it. A real mate. I mean, when a relationship's over, it's over, right? No point hanging on to it if it's making you both miserable.'

PJ leant in closer. 'I always miss the interesting stuff. How come you never told me any of this?'

'I didn't know,' Sarah said. 'But it's fine. I mean, I was going to dump Mark anyway.'

'Why?'

The billion dollar question. Sarah froze. She wasn't ready to tell her yet. She needed more time. 'I need to wash my hands.' She dived out of her seat, towards the ladies, before Kate could stop her.

'What was all that about?' PJ asked, concerned. 'Is Sarah OK? She looks terrible. And how did you end up with Mark?'

Kate squirmed in her seat. 'It's a long story.'

'So tell it.' PJ elbowed her gently. 'I want to know what's been going on.'

'Well, if you insist,' Kate grinned. Sarah always took ages in the toilets, doing her hair. She'd been bursting to tell PJ anyway. 'Mark started giving me lifts home from college and we just clicked.' She sighed happily. 'Then one evening, he came round when everyone else was in bed . . .'

'I get the picture,' PJ giggled. 'Late night snogging session?'

Kate nodded, stirring her coffee dreamily. 'We've been meeting in secret ever since. I wanted to tell Sarah last night.'

'That's why you were looking for her at the gig?'

'I found her outside. And she was pretty embarrassed when I did.' Kate bit her lip and closed her eyes with a groan. She'd said way too much.

'What was she doing?' PJ was all curious now. 'Why was she embarrassed, Kate? Tell me.'

'I can't,' Kate cringed, pretending to read the menu. 'You'll have to ask Sarah.'

'Ask me what?' Sarah sat down again looking worried.

PJ whispered. 'What were you doing when Kate found you last night?'

'Thanks a lot.' Sarah glared at her so-called mate. 'Just drop me in it why don't you?'

'Drop you in what?' PJ was getting confused. 'Will one of you tell me what's going on?'

'We bumped into Conrad. Didn't we, Sarah?' Kate nudged her across the table. 'In fact, that's what Sarah wants to talk to you about.'

'Conrad?' PJ shuffled closer, eager for gossip. 'Why, what's he got to do with it?'

Sarah sucked a strand of her hair, nervously. 'He was there too.'

'Where?' PJ looked puzzled. Sarah wasn't making any sense.

'Outside. I only saw Kate and Mark together, because I was already out there.' She took a deep breath and just said it. 'Kissing Conrad.'

Sarah closed her eyes and waited for PJ to erupt. 'Just let me explain before you say anything, OK?' she rambled. 'We didn't plan it. It sort of . . . that is, we've been talking a lot lately and it just happened.' The words were coming out of her mouth all wrong. So much for practising. 'You know I would never do anything like this on purpose. And I feel terrible about it. Really, really terrible.'

'Sarah was brilliant when she found out about me and Mark,' Kate added quickly. 'We could have fallen out, but we talked it over, and that's probably what you two should do, right?'

'Right, because we've been friends for a long time, PJ.' Sarah paused.

PJ hadn't said a word since she'd started talking. Why didn't she just explode, or cry or something, and get it over and done with? The silent treatment was worse than a massive row. What was going on inside PJ's head? Anger, rage? Was she too upset to speak? Sarah couldn't take it. She had to know.

'Well, say something,' she burst out.

'What do you want me to say?' PJ stared down into her cup.

Sarah's eyes were filling up. This was the worst moment of her life. 'I'm sorry,' she mumbled. It was too little too late.

PJ stood up slowly, shaking her head. 'I can't believe you snogged Conrad. My boyfriend.'

She looked straight at Sarah, then suddenly leant across the table and gave her a big squeezy hug. 'That's the best thing I've heard all week,' she squealed. 'I wondered how long it would take you two to get it together.'

Sarah stared at her, stunned. PJ had obviously flipped. 'You don't understand,' she gasped, banging the table with her menu. 'Me and Conrad . . .'

'I know, I heard you the first time.'

'Well, you don't seem too upset?' Kate was amazed.

'You two are so slow sometimes. I couldn't care

less about Conrad.' PJ sat down again, opening a sachet of sugar. 'I've been seeing someone else for ages.'

Kate dropped her spoon on the floor, grasping the edge of the table in shock. 'Who?' she demanded loudly.

'Joe.'

'*Joe*!' Sarah shrieked. 'Floppy fringe Joe? The computer guy. Kate's Joe?'

'Kate's ex,' PJ corrected her, grinning.

'You and Joe are an item?' It was Sarah's turn to be confused.

'So you're not angry with me? You don't mind about Conrad?'

PJ giggled. 'You may snog him with my blessing. I mean, let's face it, Conrad's not exactly my kind of guy.' Finally, she'd found someone who was. Joe didn't treat her like a doormat, or try to smother her. He knew when to make her laugh, when to leave her alone, and even when to give her a surprise snog.

He might have been too quiet for Kate, but PJ preferred her guys that way. Independent, self-assured, in control. She didn't have to play stupid games to get what she wanted. He just understood. He was amazing. And so good-looking. Every snog was a deep and lasting brush with pleasure.

'I've just seen Joe in here,' Kate spluttered, suddenly remembering.

'Good. I told him to meet me,' PJ stood up and waved Joe over from his table.

Kate and Sarah turned to watch, in stunned silence, as he walked casually across the pâtisserie.

'What on earth do you see in him?' Kate asked bewildered. 'He's like, so boring.'

PJ hit her arm. 'Just because he didn't come running when you snapped your fingers. That doesn't make him boring. It just means he's smart.'

Kate grinned at Joe mischievously as he sat down with his arm around PJ. 'It didn't take you long to get over me,' she teased. 'I thought I'd broken your little heart.'

Joe laughed. 'You might have burst a few blood vessels.'

Especially when she'd attacked his ankles in the Pizza Palace. PJ didn't do stuff like that, thank God. Joe felt for her hand under the table. She was a much better girlfriend than Kate. And she was cute too.

'Don't look so shocked.' PJ tried to snap them out of it. 'You must have known something was going on.'

'How could we? You never tell us anything. You just kept disappearing and being all mysterious,' Sarah gasped.

'So that's why you stood us up at that footie match?' Kate was slowly piecing things together.

PJ smiled. 'That was the first day we really got

talking. And things just . . . developed from there.'
She brushed Joe's hair out of his eyes. 'Do you still
want to go to the cinema tonight?'

He nodded. 'I've got to go to the cash point
first.' He smiled at Kate and Sarah and made a
quick exit.

Kate wiped the steamy window, studying his
rear view carefully as he walked past outside. He
still had a great butt.

'So is it the real thing? Do you love each other
passionately?' she teased.

PJ sipped her coffee. 'I'm not telling you two.'

'You have to tell us something.' Sarah was
recovering fast. She moved round to PJ's side of
the table. 'I've been panicking like mad. I thought
you were going to kill me.'

'I'm not telling you anything.'

'Never mind,' grinned Kate, wickedly. 'I've been
out with Joe. I know all his secrets.'

'Not all of them.'

Kate flopped back in her seat. She had a feeling
PJ liked Joe a lot more than she'd ever let on. 'Just
wait until Mish hears about this little outbreak of
boyfriend swapping,' she said.

'Who cares about Mish?' Sarah grinned.

'And we all ended up with the guy we really
wanted, right?' said PJ.

Kate nodded. 'We should have swapped ages
ago.'

'Exactly.' PJ called the dishy waiter over to their table, so that they could all order cakes. 'I knew you two would work it out eventually. I mean, it was so obvious. You'd have to be blind not to see it.'

More red-hot reads to make you sizzle...

Girls On Tour
by Alison James

A month away training-it around Europe is just the ticket for three best buds. Travel, adventure and a life under canvas beckon and, let's face it, so do loads of tanned-up toned-up lads! Mmmmmm!

£2.99 ISBN - 0-09-925152-3

The Red-Hot Love Hunt
by Jenni Linden

When your mate's in a state over a lost love, it's time to find her a new one. Three best mates set out to help their friend secure the boy of her dreams and... find themselves falling too!

£2.99 ISBN - 0-09-925112-4

J-17

THE FIRST AND LAST WORD

The coolest mag a girl can get!

On sale 3rd of every month

Can you handle more steamy reads...?

Love Games
by Jacqui Deevoy

A school tennis exchange is the perfect excuse for some on and off court encounters. As brazen Brits meet sultry Swedes, it's guaranteed to be game, set and definite love match all round!

£2.99 ISBN - 0-09-925142-6

Double-Cross Dilemma
by Linda Sheel

What do you do when you discover your best mate's boyfriend is a two-timing double-crossing low life of the first order. Keep schtum as you know she won't believe you anyway, or tell all and risk losing your friendship? What's a girl to do?!

£2.99 ISBN -0-09-925132-9

J·17

Subscription offer
12 issues for the price of 11!

Get your fave mag delivered to your door every blimmin' month for a year and never miss a copy! How? Simply complete your details and return this coupon with your payment to *J17* Subcriptions Department, Tower House, Sovereign Park, Market Harborough, Leicestershire LE16 9EF.

☐ I enclose a cheque/postal order made payable to *J17* magazine for £16.50

Please debit my Access/Visa/Amex/Diners

☐☐☐☐☐☐☐☐☐☐☐☐☐☐☐☐☐☐

Expiry date _____ Signature _____

Date _____

Name _____

Address _____

_____ Postcode _____

Or phone the Subscriptions Orders Hotline
01858 435339
Between 9.30am and 5.30pm Monday to Friday

Offer closes 30 June 1998 and is open to UK residents only   **WA19**